"I<small>F YOU THINK I'M IN SO MUCH DANGER,</small> C<small>OLE</small>, then why did you ask me to stay?" Kira asked softly.

"I'm not sure," he answered finally. "But I imagine it's the same reason you didn't run away when you had the chance."

His eyes were so dark they held no light at all. Kira didn't mistake his meaning. Is that the deal then? You'll help me if I . . . stay?"

He smiled, the shine of white teeth playing off the bottomless black pools of his eyes and giving him an aura the other side of wicked. Kira realized she'd felt safe because she truly hadn't believed the rumors about his notorious past. She did now.

"What exactly are you offering, Kira? Are you saying that if I help you, you'll go to bed with me?"

Heat crept over her skin until her body felt as if it were on fire. She wished he'd stop staring at her like that. She wished he'd do something to put the fire out. "If that's what it takes," she answered, struggling not to back down.

Cole chuckled softly, pressing his finger softly into the soft indentation beneath her lips, parting them slightly. "We both know I could have you in my bed—with or without a promise to help you." He watched her nod grudgingly at the truth of his words, then lowered his head until his lips were almost touching hers, teasing her mouth with their heat. "I'll help you, sweet lips," he said, his voice rough. "But not for sex. . . ."

WHAT ARE *LOVESWEPT* ROMANCES?

They are stories of true romance and touching emotion. We believe those two very important ingredients are constants in our highly sensual and very believable stories in the LOVESWEPT *line. Our goal is to give you, the reader, stories of consistently high quality that may sometimes make you laugh, sometimes make you cry, but are always fresh and creative and contain many delightful surprises within their pages.*

Most romance fans read an enormous number of books. Those they truly love, they keep. Others may be traded with friends and soon forgotten. We hope that each LOVESWEPT *romance will be a treasure—a "keeper." We will always try to publish*

LOVE STORIES YOU'LL NEVER FORGET BY AUTHORS YOU'LL ALWAYS REMEMBER

The Editors

BLACK SATIN

DONNA
KAUFFMAN

BANTAM BOOKS

NEW YORK · TORONTO · LONDON · SYDNEY · AUCKLAND

BLACK SATIN

A Bantam Book / March 1994

LOVESWEPT *and the wave design are registered
trademarks of Bantam Books, a division of
Bantam Doubleday Dell Publishing Group, Inc.
Registered in U.S. Patent
and Trademark Office and elsewhere.*

*If you would be interested in receiving protective vinyl covers for your
Loveswept books, please write to this address for information:*

Loveswept
Bantam Books
P.O. Box 985
Hicksville, NY 11802

ISBN 0-553-44424-7

Published simultaneously in the United States and Canada

*Bantam Books are published by Bantam Books, a division of Bantam Dou-
bleday Dell Publishing Group, Inc. Its trademark, consisting of the words
"Bantam Books" and the portrayal of a rooster, is Registered in U.S. Patent
and Trademark Office and in other countries. Marca Registrada. Bantam
Books, 1540 Broadway, New York, New York 10036.*

PRINTED IN THE UNITED STATES OF AMERICA

OPM   0 9 8 7 6 5 4 3 2 1

I would like to acknowledge and give special thanks to Howard Siegel of the Society for Environmental Awareness, Dr. Betsy Smith, Russell McFee, and the staff at Dolphins Plus in Key Largo for the very important work they are doing and for so generously sharing their hard-earned knowledge with me.

This book is dedicated to Violet.
Thank you for making me a better writer.
(And for knowing what really happened
to Elvis.)

ONE

Cole Sinclair glanced up as the door opened. His hand stilled, the shot glass an inch from his lips. She looked about as out of place as a Sunday-school teacher at a bikers' convention, he thought, then tossed back the shot of tequila. More from habit than interest, he quickly scanned her from head to toe as she squinted into the dim interior of Repo's bar. His trained eye registered everything down to the tiniest detail, but her casual slacks, sensible flats, and yellow windbreaker only confirmed his first impression. And Repo's was not the sort of place a lady patronized, unless she wanted an advanced education in how to get down and dirty.

He rolled his shoulders lightly to loosen them up and surveyed the room. It was a typical Friday night. Thick smoke hung over the pool tables, and the raw language was second only to that on the nearby shrimp docks. But if an attractive, unescorted woman had a thirst and chose to quench it in a dive with some of Key West's more unsavory characters, it was no skin off his butt.

His break was almost over. He reached behind him for his mouthpiece and loosened the ligature. He slipped in a new reed and retightened the clamp, ignoring both the urge to see how the schoolteacher was handling invitations to "rack 'em up" with the boys and the fact that no one here gave a rat's ass when, or if, he played the sax.

He was more successful at the latter.

Maybe it wouldn't hurt to have another shot. He leaned back to lay the sax in the case at the edge of the stage. Only a slight pause in his movements belied his surprise when a soft voice called his name.

"Mr. Sinclair? Cole Sinclair?"

The voice was soft, cultured, and reached his ears easily over the raised voices and cracking ivory balls. The schoolteacher. *Now what?* He shoved the unwanted nudge of curiosity aside. Whatever she wanted, he didn't have it.

He took his time before slowly turning to face her. "No."

That caught her off guard. Good. He knew she wasn't familiar with the joint. He'd also noticed how she'd deftly avoided graphic propositions from Two-Finger Tony and Iguana Man. And she'd done it without brass knuckles or firepower. Quite a feat at Repo's. The lady was determined.

Or desperate.

He absently wondered what would have stopped her. He also wondered what shade her eyes were, but didn't care enough to find out. In fact, he was so uninterested, he tilted his chair back against the stage, then pinned her with a stare he knew would shake up Repo himself. He shot a glance at the potbellied Cuban behind the battle-scarred bar, picturing the sawed-off shotgun he kept hidden behind it. Crowd control, he called it. Repo served great tequila, but he could be one evil-tempered son of a bitch.

Cole turned his full attention on the schoolteacher. She didn't look away as he purposely let his gaze drift over her. The slight shifting of her weight indicated she wasn't quite as cool and calm as she let on, but she held her ground.

He started to tell her where the door was and what part of her anatomy he wanted on the other side of it, but she chose that moment to moisten her lips. He closed his mouth. It couldn't hurt to indulge himself in the cheap thrill of watching those wet lips move.

"You have to be him," she stated. "I could have sworn Miller specifically said—" She broke off as his chair slammed back down on all fours.

"Miller?" Cole didn't have to search his mind for the name. He never forgot one and knew he'd never met anyone named Miller. He didn't know who she was, either, but apparently at least two people knew who and where he was. In his old line of work those were bad odds. He couldn't ignore the warning sensation that made the back of his neck prickle. He'd ignored it once before, a mistake he'd never make again. "Who are you, and what in the hell do you want?"

She started at the leashed violence in his tone. She broke eye contact, smoothing her hand over light brown hair that brushed her shoulders as she took a visible steadying breath. Squaring her shoulders, she looked at him again.

Cole had to concede her some admiration. It was a rare occasion when someone stood up to him.

"Are you or aren't you Cole Sinclair?" she asked evenly.

"Why don't you tell me what you want," he said. "Then I'll decide."

He noticed her knuckles whiten as she gripped the backrest of the chair. Determination and intimidation. Interesting opponents. He wondered which part he was going to enjoy more: winning—or the battle itself.

"I have a proposition for Mr. Sinclair."

Cole laughed. The sound was low and rough and spoke of too much bar smoke and too many tequilas. "Baby, you don't have anything I want. But I'm sure you could get some interest over there at the bar."

Now it was her turn to smile.

"So, you *are* Sinclair."

Thinking back over his smart-ass answer, he had to chalk up one for the schoolteacher. "The answer is still no."

"You haven't even heard me out." She hurried into her explanation before he could respond. "P.J., my, er . . . Well, the thing is he's missing. Miller Jantzen told me you were the one who found Toby and brought him back to Marathon. I need your services, Mr. Sinclair, and I'm willing to pay."

Someone had kicked the old jukebox, and the sudden blare of music muffled most of her words. Except for that last part. She'd shouted it so loud, he figured the whole bar heard. *So, the lady wanted him so bad, she was willing to pay for it?* Unbidden, images of those full lips drifting over his body burned hot and bright inside his head. He doubted she was looking for that particular service, but he had to admit the possibilities were almost tantalizing enough to pursue. Almost.

"Sweetheart, the only work I do for pay or play is done with this sax. You want to get serviced, see Repo at the bar. He'll line the guys up." A lazy smile curved his lips. "Even without the cash incentive, I doubt you'd have to do more than name your man and your position and get all the . . . ah, servicing you need." He leaned forward, his gaze heated and predatory, victory in sight. "And if that isn't enough, then you come back to me. But I'll warn you, you take me on, and it won't be over till I say it's over."

Cole dropped his gaze to the table and reached for the bottle of tequila. He knew from the shock and anger that had crossed her face that he'd gone further than necessary to prove his point. But he figured he'd done her a favor. He doubted she'd be frequenting Repo's establishment anytime in the next century. Hell, she should thank him for it. He reached for the shot glass.

Slender fingers closed tightly around his wrist, trapping it against the table. He went completely, totally still. He instinctively drew into himself, searching for and eventually finding the control she'd neatly robbed him of with her surprise move. He barely registered the fact that she wasn't all that soft or weak, that part of her palm was callused, and her grip was fairly strong.

His muscles coiled into tight springs of tension. After the explosion two years ago, he'd dealt with the devastation and guilt by creating an impenetrable wall around him. It had taken a few broken bones and a pint or two of blood to get the point across, but he'd gotten what he needed. Space. A lot of it.

He stared at her hand on him. It had been a long, long time since anyone had touched him.

"Please." Her voice was low and close enough that he could feel the intensity of her request.

The need to yank his arm away was sudden and overwhelming. Using considerable restraint, Cole kept his arm still, hoping he wouldn't betray the cost by shattering the glass gripped tightly in his hand. He shifted his gaze from her hand on his arm to her face and received another blow.

Her eyes were gray. Not a flat, dull, uninteresting gray. Instead, they looked like shattered diamonds; as if hundreds of tiny shards of dark and light had been tossed up and fallen in a mosaic pattern that hinted of color, but no matter how deeply he searched, he found none. He couldn't shake the feeling that he'd just looked into the eyes of his soul. "It must be the Cuervo," he muttered.

He forced his gaze away, purposely letting it drift to her mouth. This he understood. Full, wet, inviting. He knew just what to do with lips like hers. He was barely a tongue's length away from tasting them. They were slightly parted. His mouth watered. He needed another drink.

When she finally spoke, her voice was taut, the fine tremor more noticeable. "You can threaten me all you want. But the fact is you are my last hope. And I'll be damned if I'm leaving without you at least hearing me out."

Cole leaned closer to her until his mouth almost brushed against her ear. "Sweet lips, if I'm your last hope, then you'd better say your prayers."

She jerked back. Her diamond eyes looked more

like hard chips of ice. "Call me 'sweet lips' or 'baby' again, and you'll be saying yours," she shot back. "My name is Kira. Kira Douglass."

Cole arched a brow, truly amazed at her continuing show of bravado. Maybe she needed a lesson in just how dangerous it was to play with explosives. Not betraying his intentions by so much as a blink, he let go of the glass and flipped his wrist over, trapping her hand under his, all in the space of two seconds.

He lifted her hand up to his chin. With her weight on her other hand, if she moved, she'd fall against the table and him. He rubbed his thumb slowly over her rapid pulse. "Do I make you nervous, *Ms. Douglass*?" He watched as her eyes widened and her pupils rapidly dilated. "Nod yes."

Visibly wary, she still managed to keep her eyes locked with his. Very slowly, she dipped her chin.

"Good. I hate to be lied to. Remember that." His thumb drifted up across her palm to the base of her fingers. He slowly traced the ridge of calluses on her palm. "You didn't get these from grading papers," he murmured distractedly, surprised he'd given voice to the thought.

Confusion filtered through the wariness in her eyes, and she shook her head. "I'm not a teacher."

Yes. Yes, you are, was his immediate thought. *You've taught me that I can be made to feel again.* He didn't appreciate the lesson.

"You're hurting my wrist."

He'd felt her flinch and released her before she'd finished speaking. She stood and rubbed her wrist lightly, her expression accusing.

"I warned you I played rough."

"Point taken. I still need your help."

Damn, she was stubborn. Cole briefly considered picking her up and removing her bodily from the bar. But holding her in his arms didn't seem a very wise move at the moment.

Well, if she wouldn't leave, he would.

He pushed his chair back, fully intending to walk away without another word. But he made the mistake of looking at her again, and the words just tumbled out. "I can't help you."

"You have to."

"Listen, sweet li—" She actually raised her brow at him, which earned her a surprised lift of his own. Her unpredictable responses made him want to taunt her, tease her, just to see what she would do or say next. He shook that thought right out of his head.

"*Ms. Douglass*, the only thing I *have* to do is get up on this poor excuse for a stage and play some music." Cole stood, picked up his sax, and started to walk away.

"You found Toby Jantzen, right?"

He kept walking, but the name clicked in his brain, and he paused. Toby Jantzen. Yeah, he remembered. Dammit. He turned to face her. "Young kid, dark brown hair, kinda slow." She took a step around the table toward him, her expression animated. He should have kept walking.

"Yes! He's one of my students. His brother, Miller, told me about you. Said you played sax in a club in Key West. I've been in every dive here looking for you. I need you to help me rescue P.J."

"Look, I don't track down lost kids. I found Toby picking through the garbage out back late one night and convinced him that maybe he'd get a better meal from his folks. End of story."

"Toby doesn't speak," she shot back, making it obvious she knew the story wasn't quite so simple. "And he must have been in a highly agitated state when you found him. Yet you managed to calm him down and get him home. That, along with some other things I found out about you, make you the only man qualified to help me. As I said, I'm willing to pay."

He stared at her. What was he was doing still standing here? Why couldn't he walk away from her? He had no desire to help her. Take her to bed maybe. Find out if the body underneath the shapeless pants and jacket could possibly be as sexy as her eyes and that mouth.

He gave himself a hard mental shake. She was not the woman for an uncomplicated roll in the sack. Yet thoughts of taking their battle of wills to a sexual playing field lingered, seducing him, exciting him, frustrating him.

A contradiction suddenly occurred to him. "You aren't a teacher, yet you say Miller is a student of yours."

"I'm not a teacher."

He arched a brow at her inconsistency.

"I operate a school for children with learning disabilities. Miller and Toby have both been enrolled there."

Cole considered her explanation. "What other things?"

"You mean, what else do I do?"

"No. You said you learned a few 'other things' about me. What is it I've done to make you want me?"

Amazingly, she blushed. Or maybe, given the dim lighting and her tanned skin, he just sensed it. That scratchy sensation skittered across his neck again. But if she knew something about his past, he had no choice but to find out.

"Tell me," he commanded softly, stepping closer until she had to arch her neck to look him in the eyes. He'd meant to intimidate her, but it wasn't until she took a small step back that he realized he'd expected—hoped?—she wouldn't be. He was enjoying this too damn much. He closed the space she'd created. "You aren't leaving until I'm satisfied."

Her eyes widened, but she remained silent. He could feel her soft breath against his chin. The diamond glitter of her eyes was almost swallowed by the swiftly dilating pupils. His gaze dropped to her mouth, and without thinking, he tilted his head down to hers. Her swift intake of breath yanked him to his senses.

He abruptly turned and sat at the table he'd vacated moments ago. Stretching his leg under the table, he kicked the chair on the other side out a few inches. "Sit down." When she didn't immediately move, he inclined his head to the empty chair. "You wanted to talk."

She shot him a tight look, but she sat down.

"What other things?" he repeated.

She studied her hands for a moment, then looked up at him. "I asked around. I have a few friends down here, and I tried to find out where you lived. But I came up empty. Miller only knew that you played the sax somewhere in Key West. I don't even know how he knew that much, but that was all I could find out."

"You pumped a kid for info about me?"

"No!" Lowering her voice, she added, "I wouldn't do that. But Miller used to accompany his brother to his classes, and for weeks after Toby was found, you were all Miller talked about. To him you were like a superhero or something."

Damn her, Cole thought. Damn her to hell. And damn him for allowing her to breathe life back into him just so she could rip it apart with one word: "hero."

When he spoke, he kept his voice flat. His tone was chilling. "One thing I am not, and never will be, is a hero."

"I realize that," she replied without hesitation. "In fact, I was counting on it."

Amazement warred with anger. Cole fought and maintained his blank expression. She squared her slender shoulders, and her tongue darted out to wet her lips. He had a sick feeling she was about to put his vow to the test.

"I know boys love to exaggerate. But when P.J. turned up missing over a week ago, I didn't know what to do. I hoped I could get him back on my own, but that's not possible. I need help. A special kind of help. I remembered Miller's endless tales and thought of you."

"Miller said I was a sax player. He's right. What gave you the impression I could give you this 'special help'?"

"I need someone who can guide a boat through the reefs and waterways around the Keys at night."

"You need someone who—" He bit off the words with an oath. Jesus, the woman could teach guerrillas a few things about the element of surprise. Between clenched teeth, he said, "So?"

"I heard you might know something about that."

"From who?"

"Locals. Some of the older conches."

Cole knew the conches, as the longtime Key

West residents were called, could have spread some tales about him, but he also knew they didn't know anything that represented a threat to him. "Doesn't this P.J. have parents to look out for him? Why are you doing this?" Another thought struck him, and he leaned forward. "Is he your son?"

"No," she answered quickly. "P.J.'s parents . . . aren't around. He was . . . is, in my care."

Cole leaned back again. Instinct told him she was lying—or at least not telling the entire truth. He believed the kid wasn't hers, but too many things didn't add up.

Definitely time to bail out.

Kira Douglass wasn't some shadow from his past come forth to threaten him. She was no threat at all. He resisted the urge to scratch the back of his neck.

"Then I suggest you get the police to help you out."

He stood and walked away, vowing nothing short of a bullet through his heart would stop him this time. He'd gone a few feet when he thought he heard her say something. He kept right on moving, telling himself he was too far away to have heard her soft voice.

It must have been his imagination, otherwise he'd have sworn she'd said, "If I call the police, they'll kill P.J."

❖————❖

Kira pressed her palms against the small cocktail table, the scratched surface biting at her skin. She watched Cole walk away without so much as a glance or good-bye. Her immediate reaction was to drop her head to her arms and cry. She fought it down.

What had she been thinking? She should have had more patience, been less defensive. A man like Cole, all dark looks and rough edges, was probably used to women begging for the honor of falling at his feet, and she'd all but told him to go bark at the moon. So what if the man was a Neanderthal? Right now, P.J. was more important than her misguided pride or even her integrity. She'd blown it big time.

For the first time in hours she became keenly aware of just how exhausted she was. Another sleepless night had been followed by one of her most emotionally draining days ever. Then she'd driven several hours in bumper-to-bumper U.S. 1 traffic from Marathon to Key West. It had been after nine by the time she'd started her hunt. She'd traipsed through five other backstreet bars and waded through proposals so slimy her skin had crawled. Repo's had been the last bar on her list. The abundance of motorcycles clustered in the side lot had done little to fire up her sorely depleted confidence.

She squinted at the neon clock cleverly encased in a Lucite beer label behind the bar. It was almost one o'clock in the morning. She had to be back at the institute in less than six hours.

She allowed herself a heavy sigh. Cole Sinclair, when she'd finally found him, was even more dangerous than she could have possibly imagined. Dark, lethal, ruthless. Those were the words that had come to mind when she'd first spotted the solitary figure sitting by the stage. She hadn't exactly known what to expect. A musician who happened to be a retired smuggler? Or a renegade who happened to play the sax? One glance at him—from his long hair, all loose and wild, the same black shade as the stubble shadowing his razor-edge jaw, to the latent power of the rangy physique sprawled with deceptive laziness in the small chair—and she'd known she'd found her man. *Her man.*

She shivered as she recalled the way he'd raked his midnight gaze over her, his manner as casual and lazy as his posture. But she knew he hadn't missed a thing. And he had an attitude that suggested he'd as soon shoot her as talk.

She'd reminded herself that she'd counted on him having those very traits. What she hadn't counted on was the sensual impact that particular package could have when combined in the form of Cole Sinclair. She preferred safe and secure. Dark and dangerous never turned her on. "Never say never," she muttered ruefully.

She was startled from her thoughts by the sound of a microphone being adjusted. She looked up to see Cole slide onto a wooden stool and drop a heavy leather strap over his head and shoulder. Her breath caught in her throat, and she found herself watching helplessly as his big hands made adjustments to the burnished sax and fiddled with the mouthpiece. She wished fervently she'd ordered a drink. Her throat was suddenly parched.

He looked even more forbidding two feet higher off the ground. A cynical smile lit the corners of her mouth. He probably enjoyed making people look up to him. He leaned over and blew into the microphone. Lord, but the man even breathed with raw sex appeal.

"Evenin'," he muttered. His gaze stayed focused on his fingers, which rubbed back and forth over the keys of the sax. He didn't seem to care what the audience, such as it was, thought. And a quick scan of the motley crowd told her the feeling was apparently mutual. Was he that bad a musician?

Kira felt the tension coil tighter in her stomach as the moment of silence stretched out. Then he wet his lips and inserted the mouthpiece. She gripped the edge of the table. It surprised her how badly she wanted to hear him play.

Leave, her brain commanded. Just get up and walk out.

Two things kept her in that wobbly vinyl chair.

The first was the realization that she had no alternative. Without Cole, P.J. was as good as dead, and everything she'd worked so hard to achieve would come to an end. But the second reason was even more compelling.

He began to play.

For the next twenty minutes Kira listened to him empty his heart and soul into that sax. She hadn't thought he had that much of either to give. Raw and vital, his music shocked her with its depth and power. He tugged emotions from so deep inside of her, she wasn't aware she had them. His compelling eyes were hidden behind tightly closed eyelids fringed with thick black lashes, his face contorted as much with emotion as with the effort of forcing air into the sax. Her throat tightened as she heard the unspoken words to his music play clearly in her head. Words expressing unbearable pain and gut-wrenching sorrow. She'd never felt so connected to someone, as if he alone understood what it had been like for her to suffer such a devastating loss.

She squeezed her eyes shut, as if removing him from sight would erase the bond that his music forged with her. The last note hung in the air for what seemed like eternity.

When Kira managed to fight the burning sensation in her eyes long enough to chance looking at him without tears spilling down her cheeks, he was gone.

No one clapped or even seemed to notice he'd played, but she didn't care. She was too busy scanning the room, hoping to see his shaggy black head and broad shoulders pop through the crowd. But he was nowhere to be found. Surely he would come back to his table. She glanced toward the speaker where she'd spied his sax case earlier.

It was gone.

The strength she'd been fighting to sustain for the last several hours finally took their toll, and she let her head drop to rest in her folded arms.

How could she have become so caught up in his music that she'd forgotten her reason for being here? P.J. was out there somewhere, alone, scared, and disoriented. Her whole program was ready to self-destruct, and she'd spent the last of her energy fighting back tears over the haunting pain expressed in an outlaw's music.

No! She couldn't let Cole Sinclair just walk away. She pushed her head off her arms, determination flowing through her again.

She forced her tired brain to think logically. Repo had to have hired Sinclair. He would know where Cole lived. She'd simply harangue him until he told her, or, worst case, she'd pay the man for the information. She mentally calculated how much cash she was carrying, then glanced behind the bar at the imposing dark-skinned bartender. She'd seen him respond earlier when someone had shouted, "Repo." He more closely resembled the bikers on the other side of the bar than an entrepreneur. She pushed her chair back. It was either face Repo or lose P.J. forever.

Not much of a choice, but in the end, an easy one.

She walked as nonchalantly to the bar as she could, choosing a spot in the rear corner where the lone waitress—when she could be bothered—picked up her drinks. She'd purposely picked it in hopes that she wouldn't attract anyone's attention other than Repo's.

She quickly found out she was wrong.

TWO

Her first hint was the foul smell of old whiskey being breathed against her cheek. Her second clue was the iguana.

"Hey."

She swallowed hard. A chirping sound reached her ears, and she steadfastly ignored it. But morbid curiosity being what it was, she darted a quick peek from the corner of her eye. Her lunch rose up in her throat. The man next to her had just dangled a live cricket over the darting tongue of a two-foot-long iguana presently making itself right at home on top of the bar.

"Buy you a beer?"

She'd avoided him earlier but knew her luck had just run out. Struggling to maintain a calm facade, she suddenly realized that Iguana Man, as the tattoo on his neck proudly proclaimed him to be, might be able to answer a few questions about Cole.

"No, thank you," she said, proud of her polite tone.

"Cricket?" With yellowed fingertips the man dangled the shiny creature directly in front of Kira's mouth.

She couldn't hide her revulsion and had to clutch the bar to keep from screaming. She wasn't afraid of insects; at least as long as she didn't have to get up close and personal with one. Realizing he was enjoying her reaction, she ground her teeth into a smile. "Thanks, but I'm trying to cut down. Aren't they supposed to be plant-eaters, anyway?"

The man hooted, revealing rotting brown teeth— what there were of them—almost as nauseating as the idea of crickets for bar munchies. Summoning her control, she turned to him, but her question about Cole died on her lips when he shoved the iguana in her face.

"This here's Elvis. And he don't eat no sissy food. I trained him to like his meals alive and kicking . . . like me." The man cackled, the sound chillingly unbalanced. "Give the lady a kiss."

On command, the iguana's serpentine tongue darted out and lashed the corner of her mouth. That did it. She shoved it away, stumbling off of her stool. "Get that . . . that *thing*, out of my face!"

She instantly realized her mistake.

Iguana Man turned on her, his tiny brown eyes narrowing further in his fury. "Nobody insults Elvis."

He scooped up his pet, then reached out and snagged her arm as neatly as Elvis had the cricket. He dragged her from the bar, his grip amazingly strong for such a skinny man.

"Stop! I'm sorry. Let me go!"

He kicked a few chairs out of the way in front of the ancient jukebox and yanked her arm hard enough to make her stumble against him. She had to force herself not to gag. What had she gotten herself into? she thought dazedly. It wasn't until he pushed her head against his foul-smelling shirt that she collected her wits enough to struggle.

"Yeah, baby, rub on me." He laughed coarsely and clamped her even tighter against his bony chest. He'd draped the iguana around her neck, the beast's tongue darting repeatedly in front of her face.

It became too much. She might have lost control of her fate where P.J. or the institute were concerned, but she damn well didn't have to endure another second of this lunatic and his reptilian side-kick pawing and licking at her.

She shifted her weight onto one foot as much as possible, then yanked her other knee up as hard as she could. It connected with air. *How had she missed?* In the next instant Iguana Man's arms spun away from her, sending her reeling across a nearby table. She sprawled across a half-full ashtray and some wadded-up napkins. She had no idea what had happened to Elvis. All thoughts of the reptile's fate fled when she heard a low growl followed by the sickening thud of flesh connecting with flesh. Someone groaned, and she managed to roll over in time to see her dance partner sink to the floor in a boneless heap.

She barely had time to absorb the scene before she found her arm again imprisoned in an iron fist. Reacting on instinct, she lashed out with her free hand, intending to claw and scratch her way out of there if necessary. A big fist trapped her hand in midswing, and she was hauled up against a chest that was neither foul smelling nor grimy. In fact, it was warm and hard and felt amazingly reassuring, like a safe port in a storm that had become suddenly violent.

Her sigh of relief quickly became a gasp of shock as she looked up into the gleaming black eyes of Cole Sinclair. She had to wonder if she hadn't just jumped from a sinking ship into the jaws of a hungry shark.

"I guess we do this the hard way," he said against her ear. "I'm going to let go of your hand, then we're going to walk out of here. Don't fight me. Don't even think about running away." He was so close, she could feel the tension in his jaw as clearly as she could see it. "And whatever you do, sweet lips," he whispered against her ear, "don't scream for help. Because I'm it."

His breath was hot on her neck, and she felt a

strange sensation attack her knees, turning them to the consistency of overcooked pasta. She told herself it was a normal reaction to being threatened. He dropped the hand in his fist and quickly pushed his fingers through hers, gripping her hand just hard enough to control her direction. He pushed through the crowd, pulling her along behind him. She stumbled, and he immediately stopped, which resulted in her rushing right up against his back. And his backside. A moan escaped her lips that she didn't even attempt to interpret.

"You can faint when we get outside," he tossed over his shoulder. "Let's move." He tugged her tightly against him and pushed on before she could come up with a suitable retort.

Focusing on keeping her balance, she only dimly registered the groan that came from the floor behind her. Cole must have heard it because he turned abruptly, tucking her against his chest as if it were the most natural thing in the world. More likely he was just trying to see over her head. She forced her attention to the events about to unfold behind her, and not how pleasant and secure she felt with her face squashed against his very firm chest.

"Don't try it, Iggy," he warned, his voice loud enough and hard enough to be heard over the blasting music.

"Sinclair, you son of a bi—"

Cole didn't wait to hear the verdict on his parentage; he just scooped her up in his arms and kicked open the door to the parking lot. He crossed the alley to the small lot where she'd parked her car. He knew it was hers. She was the only person presently at Repo's whose mode of transportation would have more than two wheels.

Kira had barely realized her predicament when he released her legs, letting her feet drop to the sandy lot. His arm behind her waist was the only thing that kept her from falling in a heap on his boots.

Instinct told her she was safe, at least from the leather-clad moron in the bar, but fatigue made it difficult to curb her temper at Cole's cavalier treatment of her. So what if he'd probably saved her life? That was no excuse to manhandle her out of there like a sack of potatoes.

As she pulled away from him she noticed the white ashes smeared across his black T-shirt. She looked down at herself. "Yuck," she muttered, and ineffectually brushed at the mess on her jacket. The ground-in ashtray scum only fired her anger, and she lifted her chin, intending to give him a piece of her mind. Her defiant chin became an instant captive of his large hand.

He pushed his face close to hers until they were almost nose-to-nose and growled so fiercely, she took a tiny step back, honestly considering running back into the bar.

"Do you have a death wish?"

Her eyes widened as he exerted enough pressure on her chin to turn it back and forth in a negative motion.

"Good. But I gotta tell you, for someone with brains enough to run a school, you sure as hell pull some dumb stunts. I swear I'm almost tempted to send you back to Iggy."

She yanked her chin from his hand and backed up another step. "No! Don't. Thank you for your help. I truly do appreciate it. And don't worry, nothing could make me go back in that place."

If her fervent response mollified him, she couldn't tell by looking at him. His chest was moving visibly, though he wasn't short of breath. And he was staring at her in a way that was starting to make her very uncomfortable. She backed up another step until her rear end bumped against her car. Nervously stuffing her hands in the pockets of her windbreaker, she encountered her keys and a crumpled piece of paper that she'd used to scribble down the list of bars.

She knew she'd been given another opportunity to plead her case, but it was hard to think coherently with him glaring at her like that. She fought the urge to tear her gaze from his to collect her wits, afraid if she even blinked, he'd disappear again.

"Your music is incredible," she blurted, nerves making her say the first thing she could think of.

Apparently that caught him off guard, because for a split second, he forgot to glare at her. Taking this as a good sign, she pursued the unlikely conversational gambit. "You really surprised me," she said honestly. Afraid she'd insulted him, she added, "I don't think I've ever been so . . . so . . ." She lost her train of thought at the sudden flash of interest that blinked out of his midnight eyes before his expression once again became a shuttered mask.

"Ever been so . . . what?" he asked quietly, his voice low and rough.

Maybe it was the lack of blaring music and rattled confusion, or maybe breathing the tropical night air after all that smoke had made her light-headed. Whichever, his softly spoken words had a stunning effect on her equilibrium. *Did he really care what she thought?* "I don't think I've ever been so moved," she said softly, sincerely.

This time she knew she hadn't imagined the flash of awareness. Instinctively, she took a step toward him. For a split second she actually had the crazy urge to reach out and touch him, to place a light caress on his arm or his cheek. Her hand was out of her pocket before she realized the absurdity of the notion. The very last thing a man like Cole Sinclair needed was reassurance or comforting. And given his reaction the one and only time she'd initiated contact with him, he especially didn't want it from her.

It went against her nature and profession not to pursue the increasingly intriguing puzzle he presented. But right now, her only concern had to be getting P.J. back.

"Did you come back because you wanted to talk to me? Have you changed your mind about helping me?"

"Is that what you were doing with that sorry son of a bitch in there? Asking for his help?"

"Of course not. At least not how you mean." She swallowed another dose of the sultry salty air. "I only went up to the bar because I thought I could bribe Repo into telling me where you lived. I was going to—" She broke off when he began to laugh, or at least she assumed that's what that low, raspy sound raking her nerves was. "It's not funny! I was almost force-fed a live insect! And it wasn't my idea to have that iguana try to stick his tongue down my throat. I'm sorry he took it the wrong way, but what did you expect me to do?"

Cole's laughter eventually faded, but all the anxiety, embarrassment, tension she'd endured had frayed her patience and common sense to a slender thread. His condescension over what she'd thought of as incredible bravery on her part snapped it.

She stepped forward and jabbed a finger in the air an inch from his chest. "For your information I do not get my jollies out of slinking into sleazy dives and begging strange men for help. And you didn't exactly make it easier. I only wanted to ask you a simple question, and you acted like . . ."

Her voice faded as her anger turned to stunned amazement. He was actually smiling at her. A real smile. With a full set of white teeth and curved lips and everything. Her heart banged twice—hard—then stopped. Lord, with his features relaxed and so . . .open, the change was incredible. He was downright gorgeous. The effect was far more lethal than when he'd pinned her with his meanest glare.

"It's been my experience that the more important a thing is, the harder you have to work to get it." The wonderful smile faded as he spoke. His tone didn't reveal much either. He reached over and took one of her hands. He'd moved slowly this time, giving her a chance to react, but his touch was so different, she didn't move.

Coming from him, gentleness was so unexpected, she simply stared at her hand as he raised it between them. He tilted it so the light from the single parking-lot lamp shone across her palm. He rubbed his thumb lightly across the dense ridge of calluses at the base of her fingers. "How did you get these?"

It took her a moment to get her breath and another to find her voice. "Pulling in line and nets."

His gaze connected with hers, then he shifted his attention to a point somewhere over her shoulder. If she turned her head the slightest bit, the unruly strands of his hair being tossed lightly by the breeze would catch on her lips. She remained still. But she caught the slight shake of his head before he looked back at her. His eyes were solid jet but held a gleam that, if she didn't know better, she would swear was respect. Either that or desire. She chose the former. She didn't think she'd survive the latter.

"You said your students were handicapped," he said quietly. "You teach them to fish?"

He continued to trace his thumb over her callused palm, making it hard for her to speak coherently. But his interest actually seemed sincere, and she found her lips curving slightly. Were they actually having a normal conversation? She fought the wild urge to laugh. She doubted there was any activity that when done with Cole Sinclair would ever be considered bland or unexciting enough to be called normal.

"No, we don't fish. Actually, what we are doing with the kids has a lot to do with why I need you."

He instantly dropped her hand, and Kira felt as if she'd been cast adrift at sea with no anchor. His face was once again an implacable mask. She had an almost uncontrollable urge to grab for his hand, wanting desperately to see the more approachable Cole again. Somehow, when he'd been touching her, she'd felt for the first time as if this whole mess might just be cleared up. That he would take care of everything.

She didn't know what she'd said to slam the walls back into place. She'd thought, given his past help with one of her students, that mentioning the children would encourage his curiosity. She clenched her hands into tight fists and looked up into eyes totally lacking emotion. Sensing this was her last chance, she gave up her last shred of pride. "Please, Cole. I'm begging you. Name your price. I'll find a way to pay it. But you have to help me." Her nerve running out, she ended on a whisper. "There is no one else."

He stared at her for the longest time, drawing out the moment until she thought she'd either scream or be sick.

He tilted her chin until her eyes met his. Breathing became impossible. Rational thought, a thing of the past.

"Kira Douglass," he murmured, then leaned closer, his mouth so close, she could taste the tang of alcohol on his breath. "You have a lot to learn about self-preservation."

She parted her lips, wanting—needing—to say something, anything that would convince him. But before her words could form, he shook his head, and she pressed her lips shut.

"Your car?" He nodded to the small compact behind her.

She was so badly distracted by his mouth, the shape of his lips, and the way they moved when he

spoke that she simply nodded. He stepped away from
her, and with the return of some personal space, she
found her hope begin to build. Had he changed his
mind after all? She wanted to ask if there was a
quiet place where they could talk, but again he cut
her off.

"Get in, lock all the doors, and get out of here
as fast as you can."

Her mouth dropped open. He had an irritating
tendency to order her around. But the crush of disappointment was even more overwhelming. She stared
at him, unable to think of a single thing to do or say
as her time with him ran out.

He uttered a succinct oath and stuck out his
hand. "Give me your keys."

That brought her back. "What?"

"Either give them to me or get them yourself.
But make up your mind quick." He glanced back
across the street at Repo's. "I'd say you have less
than two minutes."

"Before what?" She raised up on tiptoes to look
over his shoulder. She didn't see anything out of the
ordinary. She turned back to Cole. "Why do—"

He heaved a sigh and raked his hand through
his hair, making the wild strands flare around his
head. "For once, would you please just do as I
say?" Apparently deciding as he spoke the futility of
the request, he uttered, "Aw hell, gimme that." He
snatched her purse from her shoulder, grumbling,

"How you made it this long without getting your throat cut I have no idea," as he began digging inside the small bag.

She didn't know if it was his personal restraint he was referring to, but she quickly decided against asking for a clarification. Still, she somehow knew he meant her no harm. "If you don't want to help, just say so," she said irritably. "Just give me my purse back. I assure you I can take it from there."

His head whipped up, and he pinned her with such a hard gaze, she dropped her hand. "Do you have any idea how many times tonight you could have become a statistic?"

She fought hard but kept her gaze steadied on his. She wanted to ask him why he cared what happened to her. "The keys are in my jacket pocket." His eyes dropped to her hips, and she quickly dug her hand in the pocket and produced the small ring. "See?" She held out a hand for her purse, her eyes challenging him to comment on the slight tremble that shook her fingers.

He tossed her the purse, then snagged the keys in midair as she dropped them instinctively to grab her straw bag. He thrust the largest one in the lock. After yanking the door open, he turned back to her, the key dangling from his fingers. "Get in." Now it was his gaze doing the challenging.

Not daring to so much as brush her skin against his, she flattened her palm and reached for the key ring. She quickly slid into the car and blindly stuck the key in the ignition, incapable of more than a mechanical action. Her only thought was to put as much distance between her and Repo's bar, Key West, and most important, Cole Sinclair, as fast as she could.

She reached out to yank the door closed, but he grabbed the frame just before it shut. He leaned down, and it took all her self-control to keep from turning her head to face him. "What?" she asked, clenching her jaw against the sudden threat of tears. She felt his sigh against the bare skin of her neck, and her fingers tightened reflexively on the steering wheel.

"No Name Key—do you know where it is?"

Startled by the question, she looked at him and answered automatically. "Off Big Pine, right?"

He nodded. "Turn at Key Deer Boulevard and go about a mile and a half. Turn right at the green sign for No Name, cross the bridge, and look for a sign to Sandy's pier. There's one houseboat, mine. Stay in your car until I get there."

Her eyes widened as she scrambled to put meaning to his words. "What did you just say?"

"You heard me." He looked over his shoulder for several seconds, then back at her. "And if you've ever done one smart thing in your life, you'll forget I ever said it. You'd better get out of here."

"Not on your life."

"Yeah, well, that's not worth much."

"It is to me."

He studied her face for a long moment, then stood up and shut the door. She was about to roll down the window to ask him if his invitation was still open, but he smacked his palm twice against the roof of her car and took off down the alley. She glanced in her rearview mirror long enough to see him duck behind the back of Repo's ramshackle building.

Less than a minute later the front door burst open and half a dozen men spilled out, their heads whipping back and forth as they quickly scanned the area. One man stepped forward, and she caught the glint of silver in his hand. Even at her distance, she knew it was Iggy. And he was carrying a knife.

"Sinclair!" he bellowed so loudly, she heard him even with her windows rolled up. "What in the hell did you do with Elvis?"

Oh, Lord. Cole had known they'd come looking when Iggy finally came around and realized his beloved iguana was missing. Cole must have known the search for the reptile would delay them. He'd even tried to warn her, but she'd been too bull-headed to realize it. What *had* Cole done with it? she wondered, figuring there couldn't be too many great hiding places for a two-foot-long iguana.

Cole! "Oh my God," she whispered. He'd gone back there to face them. Alone.

She didn't want to take off and leave him, but an equally loud voice told her he could take care of himself and that she'd only make matters worse. She gunned the gas and backed out, hoping at least to draw their attention away long enough to give Cole more time.

It worked. Too well, judging by the fact that they turned en masse toward the small lot and her car. She assumed they meant to chase her on foot and threw the car into first gear. They pursued her for a few yards, then turned back, racing to the lot on the other side of the building and clambering onto a row of gleaming, nasty-looking motorcycles.

Uh-oh. She slammed her foot down on the pedal, sand and gravel flying in her wake. She glanced into the rearview mirror, expecting to see a dozen Harleys hot on her tail. What she actually saw made her mouth drop open in amazement, quickly followed by an astonished whoop of laughter.

The first bike had moved forward only to topple over, starting a chain reaction that made the huge machines look like nothing more than a bunch of mutant dominoes. Apparently someone had chained them together. And she knew without doubt who that someone was.

She pumped her fist in the air. "All right!" Her smile faded. *Where was Cole?* She got her answer a split second later when a loud roar zoomed past her, the power of the machine making her car vibrate. She glanced around just in time to see Cole's lean body hunched over a sleek black bike as it raced off into the night. Without another look at the bar, she followed him.

She'd lost Cole's taillight by the time she'd reached Route 1. She felt strangely abandoned, even though frequent checks in her rearview mirror told her no one had followed them from the bar. She'd gone past Boca Chica and Shark Key and was crossing through the Saddlebunch Keys before she questioned the possible motives behind his invitation. She'd assumed he'd asked because he'd decided to help, or at least give her a chance to explain further. But maybe that was the last thing on his mind.

A shiver raced along her spine. He'd been so gruff with her about being alone in the bar and so concerned about her safety. Certainly a man who'd put himself at risk to rescue her from apparent danger wouldn't have any plans of seduction or . . . worse. *Would he?*

Was she as naive as he'd accused her of being? Maybe he figured he was owed a little something for all the trouble she'd put him through tonight. The more she thought about it, the more nervous she became. She was actually going to a houseboat on a tiny mostly deserted key, alone, to meet a man reputed to have done all sorts of illegal things. Not to mention he had a bad-boy appeal so seductive it all but shouted, "Trespass at your own risk."

Her foot relaxed on the gas pedal as all sorts of images sprang to mind. His music, almost tangible with pain, echoed through her head as clearly as if she were playing it on cassette. Her heart responded again as it had in the bar. *What had happened to put that kind of music into his soul?*

No. Don't start thinking of him that way. If anyone could take care of himself, it was Cole Sinclair. The scene at the bar had more than proven that. She shook her head, clearing it of all images save one. *P.J.*

That was all it took. She pressed her foot firmly back on the gas. "I don't know what you have in mind, Cole Sinclair," she said to the dark road ahead. "But by the time we get done, you are going to help me find P.J."

By the time she crossed the channel between Little Torch and Big Pine, she'd convinced herself that she could play to his apparent weakness for lost children and damsels in distress to secure his help.

But on the heels of that plan came the unsettling image of his probable reaction when she told him everything. Much as she hated subterfuge, she'd sensed right off that her best chance was to get Cole involved in her plan before telling him the whole truth. So she'd allowed him to draw some conclusions that weren't exactly true. If he knew it wasn't a child she was asking him to rescue . . .

No, he had to be fully committed to her cause before she told him that P.J. was a dolphin.

THREE

Cole pulled off the side of the highway as soon as he crossed the Saddlebunch 2 channel. He shut his headlight off and waited in the shadows for Kira's car to go by. If he hadn't glanced in his rearview mirror as he was pulling out of Repo's, he wouldn't have known she was still there. It didn't surprise him that she hadn't listened. It irritated the hell out of him.

Her small sedan flew by moments later. He waited thirty seconds to make sure no one was following them, then pulled back onto the highway. Luckily, the late-night traffic was light, and he was able to get within sight of her car relatively quickly.

He half hoped she'd keep on going past the turnoff on Big Pine and head on across the Seven Mile Bridge back to Marathon. Now that she wasn't within arm's reach, he'd been able to go over the night's events with a clearer mind. Her request was crazy. She was crazy.

Pleading with him one minute, telling him off the next. He'd even been aware of her watching him while he was playing. That unnerved him the most. Usually when he played, the world ceased to exist. Music was both his escape and his penance. It was the only time he allowed himself to feel. It was hellish torture, but it also provided a vent, an outlet for his grief—and his guilt. And she'd known. It had been in her eyes and in her voice.

"Damn," he muttered as he turned in behind her onto Key Deer Boulevard then followed her across Bogie Channel onto No Name. He should have left after he'd finished playing. But he'd made the mistake of looking out of the back room. He saw Iggy grab her arm, and something deep inside him had snapped.

She slowed after she crossed the bridge, and he zoomed around her and led her past the small wooden sign with the word SANDY'S carved into it and a crude arrow drawn above it. He parked his bike under the single bare bulb at the end of his pier. He didn't bother locking it up. Aside from Sandy's small shack, which was situated about twenty yards away and doubled as a rental shop and a few empty boats strung up along a second nearby dock, they were alone. Completely alone.

Cole walked down the short dock and jumped

aboard his houseboat. He shouldn't have invited her. And she sure as hell had no business following a strange man all alone to such an isolated place. He intended to tell her that as soon as she came on board. He'd scooped up a handful of gym shorts and tossed them past the folding door to his bedroom before it occurred to him he was actually cleaning up for her. He raked his fingers through his hair in frustration and stalked to the small kitchen to grab a beer.

He downed half a bottle in one long pull, then rubbed the cold glass against his forehead. He didn't want to make a good impression; he didn't want to make any impression. Hopefully she'd gotten cold feet when he hadn't waited for her. To further discourage her, he'd purposely left off all the lights but a small one in the main cabin.

"Cole?" Her voice was tentative but carried easily through the screened windows.

He uttered a succinct oath, then finished the beer before answering. "Yeah, be right there."

He slid open the door to the back deck and walked out. He didn't offer her a hand, just stood there staring at her. Even in the waning moonlight he didn't miss the thrust of her small chin as she moved to climb aboard. She walked to him with the grace and balance that told him she was as comfortable on water as she was on land. He recalled her comment about pulling in nets and found himself involuntarily wanting to know more about Kira Douglass.

"I assume you didn't invite me here to stare at me all night."

He levered away from the railing and took a step toward her. "And why *do* you think I asked you here?" He purposely kept his voice low and a bit rough.

"Hopefully to talk about my proposition."

He grinned and took another step. "I don't think anyone has ever gone to so much trouble to . . . proposition me before."

She took the tiniest of steps backward, then jerked to a stop as her back bumped against the railing. "Well, given your attitude, I'm surprised anyone bothers at all."

Before he could so much as lift an eyebrow in response, she said, "Is there somewhere we could sit and talk? I'm sure if you'll just let me explain, you'll understand why it's so important."

He heard the tension and trace of desperation in her voice and felt a moment of regret for pushing her just now. But teasing Kira, watching her react, not knowing how she would, was too pleasurable to regret completely. And pleasure was a rare commodity in his life.

He slid open the door to the main cabin, unsettled by the sudden desire to see her in his home, among his possessions. Meager as they were.

She stepped quickly past him, and he got a quick whiff of her scent as her hair brushed against his chin. It was a small thing, that light, teasing scent, but unexpected after the smoky barroom. He liked it. He watched her unzip her yellow windbreaker and start to slide it off. Her shoulders were well toned and deeply tanned; the soft ribbed tank top she had on underneath did wonders for satisfying his earlier curiosity about what curves lay under the baggy surface. And oh, what curves they were. Small, but full, they'd be all silky resilience to his touch. Her crystalline gaze met his, and she quickly slipped her jacket back onto her shoulders. Her fingers hovered over the zipper, but she left it open.

He clenched his hands into tight fists against the desire to stroke his fingers down the narrow woven ridges of fabric that clung so wonderfully to her breasts. Instead he turned to the kitchen. "Can I get you a beer?"

"Um, no thanks. I have to drive the rest of the way back to Marathon tonight . . . this morning, I guess."

It was on the tip of his tongue to ask her if she intended to stay the night. No more teasing, he declared silently. Too dangerous. She was defi-nitely not the type for hit-and-run sex. He cleared his throat. "Water?"

"Yes, that would be great. Thank you."

So polite, he thought, and smiled to himself as he

stepped into the small kitchen and pulled the gallon jug of spring water out of the fridge. He dropped a few ice cubes in some glasses, filled them, and went back to her. He handed her a glass, then settled on a stool in front of the small rattan bar, resting his elbows behind him and propping his booted feet on the small cluttered coffee table positioned between him and the couch she was sitting on. "Perched" was actually a better word.

"Why haven't you called the police?"

Kira gulped and took a small sip of her water, praying it would slide past the knot in her throat. He didn't waste any time. Sitting up straight, she told herself that it was just as well. The sooner she got him to agree to help, the better. As it was, she wouldn't be getting any sleep tonight anyway. An image of Cole's lazy smile and the sound of his deep voice floating to her in the darkness flashed through her mind, and she wondered if sleepless nights would plague her for some time to come.

"I run a private institute that provides help to people, mostly children, with emotional and physical disabilities. Some of them are autistic, some have Down's syndrome, others may have cerebral palsy, learning disorders, or may be recuperating from major injuries. I get all my funding from private groups."

She took another sip and paused, but he remained thankfully silent. "In a little over one week, I'm having a sort of open house for a variety of investors that have in some way expressed interest in funding what we do. The school is very costly to run, and because our programs are still considered experimental from a scientific viewpoint, we have to rely solely on their support to keep it operating. Many of our supporters are initially drawn to us by local and national media coverage of some of our unique methods."

"And if word leaked out that one of the students in your care had turned up missing, you'd lose the supporters."

She breathed a small sigh of relief. Maybe, just maybe, getting him involved would be easier than she thought. "More or less, yes."

"I still don't understand the urgency." When she started to speak, he raised his hand to silence her. "I know you don't want the kid out there wandering around. But if the investors don't know about the missing boy, then why can't they just come and view the school and leave none the wiser? In the meantime hire a private investigator who will discreetly search for the boy."

"It's a little more complicated than that."

He'd apparently sensed her apprehension, because he let his feet thunk to the floor and bent over to rest his elbows on his knees. "Well, then, why don't you just get to the point," he said quietly, his expression making it clear he wouldn't be pushed any further. "You know where he is, don't you?"

"I, uh . . ." His eyes were so black and so focused on her, she had a hard time stringing words together. Lord, but the man was intense. "Yes. I know where P.J. is," she answered. "But I need your help to get him back."

"Where is he?"

"He's being held on an estate on a privately owned key located on the Gulf side between Ramrod and Summerland," she answered, referring to an area a few miles south of No Name.

Cole's eyes narrowed suspiciously, and she automatically leaned back against the cushions of the couch.

"This wouldn't by any chance be a custody battle?"

"No. It's kidnapping, and I want him back." She raised her hand to cut off his attempt to speak. "Police or detectives are out of the question. No one can know."

Cole scratched the back of his neck and put his empty glass on the bar. With deceptive calm he stood and walked around the small table, using his towering advantage over her to its fullest potential. She was going to have to get it through her head that he wasn't a man to play games with.

In a too soft voice he said, "Once, a long time ago, I made the mistake of not listening to my instincts. Trust me when I tell you that the result was ugly. I vowed never to make that mistake again." He bent over and rested one hand on the back of the sofa, bringing his face within inches of hers. "My instincts are telling me that something's real wrong with your story. You're either lying or not telling me the whole deal. Either way, sweet lips, you've got about thirty seconds to correct that or find someone else to help you."

The dark stubble sandpapering his jaw looked as rough as his voice was against her nerves. "If I tell you everything, will you help me rescue P.J.?"

He stared intently into her eyes, as if trying to solve some mysterious puzzle. "You aren't in a position to bargain."

His lips curved, and she doubted the positions he was thinking about had anything to do with rescuing dolphins.

"Twenty seconds and counting, Kira."

Kira. The way he said her name sent tiny jolts of awareness throughout her entire body. The way he looked at her sent giant jolts to her brain. The unholy gleam that lit the depths of his black eyes told her she hadn't been too successful in hiding that reaction. Cole Sinclair wanted her. And the mere thought that a man like Cole could desire her was strangely empowering.

Would he help if he thought it would get him

something he wanted? Namely her. In bed. Or, gauging from the taut line of his jaw, possibly right here on the couch. The image of them twined together, his big hands all over her, his lips pressed against her feverish skin, seared her brain, and she fidgeted restlessly as she fought against them. No. Stupid idea. She'd never survive something like that. Better to keep this all business.

"Ten seconds."

She didn't have a choice. Before she could explain the rest, he had to know. "P.J. isn't a child." That threw him, but at least he didn't look angry.

"Why doesn't this surprise me?" he asked the ceiling. To her, he said, "Okay, I give up. If P.J. isn't a kid, just exactly what are you asking me to help you rescue?"

"A dolphin."

Cole sank down on the couch next to her. "You want me to rescue a fish?"

Kira struggled to keep her patience in check. She'd known this wasn't going to be easy, and it was crucial that he understand. "Dolphins aren't fish, they're mammals," she began. "You'd have to see them, be with them, to understand the amazing abilities they have." She paused. Maybe there was hope. He wasn't tossing her overboard, anyway. Of course, the night wasn't over yet.

"What do dolphins have to do with your school?"

She smiled. His question seemed sincere. She

just might pull this off. "Our institute is different from others. There are several other dolphin centers in the Keys. But while all of them have some class time set aside for disabled kids, most have to rely on a heavy tourist trade to support the other work and research they do. Dr. Dolphin—that's the name of our institute—is aimed solely at helping children, and some adults, overcome their individual disabilities."

"Let me get this straight. You're telling me that the dolphins help heal the kids?" His tone made it clear that he thought her claims were at best only slightly unbalanced. "It's no wonder you're hard up for investors."

"Cole, if you could only see it. Autistic children who have been completely unreachable respond to dolphins in amazing ways. The dolphins seem to sense the neediness in the kids. The connection is awe-inspiring."

"I'd think if this is as great as you say it is, money would be pouring in."

"It's not that easy. While much research has been done with dolphins privately in the last decade, their work with the disabled is still considered very experimental. We still don't know exactly why it works so well, just that it does. Much of our time and a good chunk of our resources are spent trying to convince investors we're not quacks."

Cole nodded. She understood; most people were

skeptical at first and needed time to absorb it all. Unfortunately, time was the one thing she didn't have. "I know if you saw them, swam with them, you'd understand."

"If you have some crazy idea of getting me to—"

She broke in. "I have no doubt I could make you a firm believer in less than an hour," she said steadily. "But I don't care what you believe as long as you agree to help. Our program will allow a large group of people who have shown an interest in contributing to come to the school. We'll give them a mini-course in dolphin education and let them sit in on several of our classes in action, as well as talk with some of our therapists and psychologists about their patients and the progress they've made."

"This is one week from now?"

"Nine days. I have to get P.J. back by then. He's been with me the longest and is the one most often profiled by the media. He works with the toughest kids and doesn't seem to mind being the focus of a lot of attention. A large number of potential investors are coming specifically to see him."

"But you have other dolphins?"

"Yes."

Cole studied her carefully for a moment, then reached out and tilted her chin toward him. "There's something else you're not telling me. What is it?"

His touch made it hard to think. "Male dolphins sometimes form very strong attachments to other males. Some pairs become virtually inseparable for years, some for life."

"I take it P.J. has a buddy."

She nodded. "Rio. He's suffering tremendously. He doesn't eat and hardly communicates with the other dolphins. When he does talk, he just calls P.J.'s name. I can only imagine what P.J.'s going through."

Cole stood up. "Whoa, lady. Now you're trying to tell me they talk?"

She tried to explain. "You've heard dolphins click and whistle, right? Remember Flipper?"

"Yeah, yeah. So?"

"Well, each dolphin has a distinct signature whistle, like a name. Other dolphins will call them out when they want to get that particular dolphin's attention."

"And you can understand the whistles?" He sounded skeptical.

Kira sighed. "We've spent years documenting and recording all aspects of our group. So, yes, the signature whistles are all on file, so to speak. And we've been able to determine whose is whose. Actually, I'm glad you asked, because it's intrinsic to my plan to get P.J. back."

Cole remained silent for a moment. "I need a beer. Want one?"

"No thanks." She sank back against the cushions. Her muscles were beginning to spasm from the torture she'd put them through this evening. But she sensed she was gaining ground. And for that she'd gladly tie herself in knots.

Kira took advantage of his absence and scanned his living quarters. Having grown up on the Gulf Coast, she'd spent some time on several houseboats. Even in the dark, she'd been able to tell that Cole's was a custom model. It was much wider than most, very upscale. That had surprised her—until she considered his previous profession might have included perks like this.

But the inside looked more like what she'd expected a man who played sax at Repo's would own. It looked as if he'd gutted the thing, then never gotten around to remodeling it. There was the small woven couch she was sitting on, a short bar with two stools, the coffee table, and a well-worn easy chair over in the corner with a wall-mounted lamp angled strategically to the side.

Aside from the doors leading to the deck, there was a folding door to her right and one straight ahead. Since she knew that one led to the kitchen area and presumably the front of the boat, she assumed the other led to his bedroom. She immediately wondered what it looked like, what kind of bed he slept on. The resulting images made her quickly search for something else to study.

She glanced around the main cabin again and realized why it seemed so stark. There was the standard bachelor clutter. Battered deck shoes heaped on

the floor by the sliding door, the occasional empty beer bottle, and a few dog-eared copies of *Life*
magazine. But there were no mementos. No photos, nothing personal placed anywhere. Not even
a print adorned the walls. She noticed a scattering of holes in the wall as if someone had tried
to hang a picture half a dozen times in the same
spot. Odd.

There was no television either, only a small ste-
reo component system behind the bar. Either he
didn't spend much time here, or he found some
other form of entertainment.

Her gaze zoomed back to the bedroom door. Yes,
she could easily picture the sort of entertainment
Cole might indulge in to while away the daylight
hours. A frown crossed her face.

She yanked her gaze away. It fell on the easy
chair in the opposite corner, and she saw that the wall
behind the chair was actually a built-in bookcase. The
shelves were packed, books crammed every which way
in order to make room for them all. Apparently, he
read a lot.

Curious about what books would attract a man
like Cole, she stood up, planning to investigate. But
hearing his booted feet on the floor, she forced herself to sit back down.

"What happens if you don't get him back?" he
asked calmly as he strolled back in the room.

Kira felt a sharp pull in the vicinity of her heart,

and her curiosity was temporarily forgotten. "If P.J. is reacting like Rio, there is a very good possibility they will both die."

His expression didn't change. "And your school?"

"If we don't get the funding, the school closes. As it is, most of the doctors and therapists volunteer their time, or are paid by their patients' families. But the institute pays for my trainers and core staff, as well as the enormous cost of the care and maintenance of the dolphins and the facility."

Cole sat back on the stool and leaned against the bar. "Not to mention your salary."

"That is not—"

He talked right over her outraged response. "So, you think the police are a bad move. Okay. But why me? Why not someone who knows something about dolphins?"

"If that was all I needed, my staff and I could handle it. But the situation requires more than our skills if we are going to pull it off."

"This has to do with the running-the-boat-at-night deal you mentioned, I take it. Again, why me?"

Kira nervously rubbed her hands up and down her thighs. "The man who kidnapped P.J. is very wealthy. I think he's penned P.J. in a private cove on his island. I need someone who knows the area and can guide the boat through the reefs and around the keys in the dark without running aground. Or being noticed."

Cole's eyes narrowed at the implication. He set his beer down and crossed the room to the couch. He stared down at her for a moment, then reached for her elbow to pull her up. There was a bare inch of space between them, but she didn't avert her gaze or try to get him to release her. Damn, but the lady had guts. Or she was desperate. He silently acknowledged that many times one had much to do with the other.

"And what exactly do you think I've done to gain that type of knowledge?" His tone was soft, but there was an unmistakable lethal edge to it.

She took a breath, and he found his eyes drawn to the pulsing skin on her neck. Just when he thought she wouldn't answer him, she said quietly, "I think you used to be a smuggler."

Cole gave up and shook his head ruefully, unable to deny her ability to face him down. He sighed. "Let's say I have a background that might have provided me with that knowledge. If that were so, how do you plan to get close enough to catch the dolphin?"

She looked up at him, with eyes so full of hope they sparkled like diamonds in the sun. For a man who led what life he had in the dark hours, her compelling radiance was blinding torture. He suppressed a groan. What in the hell was he doing with her? His gaze dropped to her lips, and he realized there was more than one answer to that question.

He let his hands drop from her shoulders. He wanted to hate feeling this way, to hate her for making him feel at all. It had been so long since anything or anyone had penetrated the walls he'd built to protect himself. But the simple truth was, it felt too damn good to walk away from. He knew he'd call himself a hundred names, all of them ugly, before this was over. But he also knew he couldn't be the one responsible for dousing the light in her eyes and killing her hope. At least not tonight.

"All you have to do is get us close without being detected," she answered. "I can take it from that point."

Cole's gaze fastened on hers again. "Alone?"

Her eyes widened a bit at his tightly voiced demand. He forced himself to relax his features a bit but didn't apologize for it. He wanted to know.

"I'm an experienced diver and trained to work underwater. I have or can get the proper equipment we need so we can work at night. All we have to do is find a way through whatever barrier he's using and then send out a recording of Rio's signature whistle. P.J.'ll come to us."

Cole studied her so closely, the back of her neck became damp. Kira curled her toes as tight as her flats would allow. She sensed he was struggling over whether or not to help her, so she tried to remain calm, making a valiant attempt to keep from breaking down and begging him again. But with all that harnessed energy of his focused so intently on her, it was difficult to remember how to breathe.

"How did you get into this line of work?"

His question startled her, but she answered it easily. "My father was a marine biologist, and I grew up helping him. I began studying dolphins in college, and when I discovered the work they were doing with children, I knew immediately this was what I wanted to do."

He nodded but took another long moment before he spoke.

"If I'm going to help you, I'll need a lot more information," he began.

His words gave her a leap of hope, and she impulsively grabbed his arm. He froze. So did she. Trapped in his gaze, she barely noticed the muscles of his forearm twitching under her fingers. For what seemed like an eternity but in reality was probably only a second or two, they stood locked in visual combat. *Damn.* She silently called herself every word she knew for idiot. She'd been so close, and then she'd done the one thing guaranteed to blow it.

She'd touched him.

In many ways he seemed a highly sensual man who wouldn't mind physical contact. But after the first time she'd impulsively touched him, she'd always let him initiate contact and noted he did so mostly to emphasize his control of the situation. Was it just her, she wondered helplessly, or any woman? Or anyone at all? His eyes glittered with fury, and she was torn between the need to try to explain and the strong instinct to run like hell.

He lowered his face toward hers, and she finally tore her gaze away. Belatedly realizing she was still holding his arm, she released him as if he'd suddenly become unbearably hot to the touch. Considering the trickle of perspiration sliding down her throat, that wasn't far from the truth.

"I'm sorry, I just . . ." She looked up as she spoke, and it hit her with the force of a gale wind that he wasn't furious with her at all. He'd dropped his gaze to her lips and was looking at them as if planning a six-course meal. A slight shudder rippled through her and caused the strangest melting sensation to slide through her inner thighs. "Cole, I really don't want—"

A slow smile curved his lips. It did terrible things to her pulse and sent the most wicked sensations skittering to pulse points all over her body.

"You do want, Kira. You want it badly. And so do I." His smile faded as he lowered his mouth to hers. His lips were firm and hot and quickly became wet as he pressed them against hers. He reached up and held her head between his large hands, tilting it slightly to allow deeper access.

Kira was consumed in sensations so intense, they simultaneously engulfed her body and seduced her mind. The pleasure of his callused palms hot against her cheeks, combined with the sweet pressure of his lips on hers, made her dizzy.

She parted her lips and felt the vibrations of his groan travel the length of her throat. There was almost a sense of desperation in the way he held her face, and the mere thought that he was in need sent her control spiraling away. She wanted badly to reach up and clutch at his shoulders for support, but she clenched her hands into tight fists at her side.

He pushed his tongue slowly into her mouth, sinuously twining it with hers, then seducing it back into his own. He tightened his hold on her tongue as if he was drinking the sweetness from it, then just as suddenly thrust his tongue back into her mouth. She knew without being told he wanted her to do the same to him. She felt a burning sensation build behind her tightly closed eyes at his silent entreaty to touch him. It was a minor concession considering he was ultimately controlling the kiss, but even such a small break in his formidable armor had a devastating effect on her. She gladly took him into her mouth and held him there tightly as she savored the taste of him.

Desire shot through her with a violence that rocked her. Never before had she wanted so much, felt so much, needed so much. Suddenly the wanting became unbearable, and she thought she might sink to the floor if she didn't hold him. At that exact moment he broke the kiss, but kept his lips only a breath from hers.

"Let that be a lesson to you, Kira," he whispered roughly. "Don't ever lie to me."

FOUR

Kira gently hung up the phone. She wanted to slam it down but refused to give Cole the satisfaction of knowing how much he'd irritated her. Besides, she still had the last feeding to do, and she barely had enough energy to stand. She wasn't about to waste any of the little she had left on Cole.

Their brief conversation echoed in her mind.

"Something's come up," he'd said. "If you want to talk, meet me at the houseboat around nine." His tone hadn't invited discussion, and she'd barely responded that she would see him then before he'd disconnected the call.

Damn that stubborn, arrogant, macho . . . If there was any other way of getting P.J. back . . . But there wasn't, and she knew it. Problem was, so did Cole. And he was apparently making sure she wouldn't forget that little fact. She'd counted on making him come to her. Hoping, despite the odds, to get him in the water with the dolphins. She also wanted the advantage of meeting him on her own turf. If only she hadn't let him kiss her last night.

Kira's face burned with humiliation at the recollection. She'd been a fool to think Cole was wrestling with some inner demon. His music and dark moods had her painting him as some sort of tortured hero. Well, he'd made it clear he was no hero. And any lingering doubts she might have had he'd effectively abolished with one kiss.

One very hot, distinctly unherolike kiss.

Kira pushed out of her chair and headed for the shed where Paul, her assistant, had left the buckets of fish for the last feeding. She quickly tied an apron over her rumpled white shorts and bathing suit. Tucking a few extra fish in one of the pockets, she headed for the pier. Thirty minutes later, nearing the bottom of the last bucket, she had managed to push away all thoughts of the disturbing Mr. Sinclair and how good his strong arms had felt around her.

She reached deep into the bucket and tossed the last piece of herring to Cutter. The dolphin snapped it up, then emitted a rapid series of clicking noises, as if begging for more of the briny treat.

"At least you're eating," she told the ever-smiling mammal. Her gaze shifted to Rio, who was swimming listlessly across the small cove to the fence at the canal, then back to the floating dock situated at the end of the other pier. The dolphin had repeated the motions over and over, day in and day out since P.J.'s disappearance. He had refused yet another full feeding. Considering it took around twenty pounds a day to keep the five-hundred-pound dolphin well fed, she was finding it increasingly difficult to ignore the nervous knot tightening in her stomach. Sighing, she picked up the empty bucket.

Cutter rose out of the water until all but his tail flukes were visible and backwalked across the surface of the water, clicking and whistling to get her attention.

"Sorry, sweetie," she called, and flipped the bucket upside down to show the dolphin that mealtime was over for now. Cutter dove under water and swam at his characteristic high speed to the edge of the dock, shooting up at the last second and sending a sheet of water cascading over Kira. Drenched but not caring, Kira laughed and licked the salty water from her lips. "You know a soft touch when you see one." Kira smiled, glad she'd allowed Paul to convince her to do the last feeding. Spending solitary time with the dolphins always cheered her up. She reached into the pocket of the apron and grabbed a handful of cigar minnows. "Here. And don't tell Paul."

"Tell Paul what?"

The familiar teasing voice of her assistant broke gently into her thoughts.

"Hey, time to punch the ol' clock. Buy a lady a beer?"

She forced a smile on her face and turned to greet him. Big and blond with a body to put any California surfer to shame, Paul Taylor had been with Kira since the start of her Dr. Dolphin Institute four years ago. At twenty-four he was almost a full decade younger than she, but despite his easy charm and devil-may-care attitude, Kira knew she couldn't have asked for a more dependable assistant.

"And risk alienating every female from here to Key West? No way," she shot back.

He casually relieved her of the empty bucket. "Did he eat?"

"Not much, maybe another pound."

"Damn."

Kira could sense the tension in him. "If it gets much worse, we're going to have to pipe him and force-feed him. But even that's chancy, not to mention temporary."

"Have you been able to dig up anything more on P.J.?"

Thoughts of Cole and the wild events of last night raced through her. The brief reprieve the dolphins had given faded away, leaving her weary and tired.

She began fiddling with her apron ties. She wanted more than anything to confide in Paul, who'd understand all the ramifications and sympathize with her problems. But she couldn't risk it, given the probability an insider had been involved.

Choosing her words carefully, she said, "I know I've been pretty vague about the details, but I'd hoped to keep you guys from worrying too much. We have so much to do—"

He placed a hand on Kira's bare shoulder and squeezed lightly. "Let me help you."

Kira smiled briefly. If he only knew how desperately she wanted to. She removed Paul's hand, giving his fingers a light squeeze before letting go. "I appreciate that, Paul, really I do. But for now, let me handle this on my own. The fewer people who get involved with this, the better."

A wariness entered Paul's eyes. "Do you know where P.J. is?" His voice had become almost urgent. He took a breath as if trying to regain control. "Why don't you tell me everything you've found out so far."

Kira tried very hard to ignore the tingling alarm that trickled down her spine. Was she just imagining the unfamiliar tone of command in his voice? Kira shook her head, as much in answer to Paul as to clear her mind. What she needed was a full night of sleep so she'd stop seeing intrigue where there was none.

"Thanks. It means a lot to know I can count on your help. But I think I've got it under control for now."

Paul studied her for a long second, and she couldn't help but wonder what was going on in his mind. Then he abruptly relaxed and shot her the wide, charming grin that had the ladies lining up to go out with him. "Okay, then. Take it easy." He turned and sauntered back toward the shed that held the extra buckets and equipment.

Kira watched him go, trying to convince herself that she should be grateful he'd let the subject drop so easily. Shivering suddenly, she crossed her arms in front of her and ran her hands over the goose bumps lining her skin. She headed quickly to her office and the dry clothes she always kept on hand. She ignored the fact that it was a balmy evening with very little breeze.

It wasn't working. Cole let the sax drop to his lap, the last notes still echoing across the water. He let his gaze drift past the railing off the back deck of his houseboat. The moon had made a striking debut a few minutes earlier, but contemplating the mysteries that lay under the water's now silvery surface did little to calm him either.

"Damn her," he muttered, letting his bare feet drop to the deck with a soft thud. He pushed out of the chair and headed inside. In a few minutes Kira would be here to fill him in on the rest of what she knew. It was information he should have gotten from her last night.

He recalled in arousing detail exactly what he had gotten from her last night. From the start her all-business attitude made him wonder if the promise of sensuality in her full lips was merely illusion.

He hadn't intended ever finding out. But he hadn't counted on her eyes looking at him as if she could see all the way to his soul. Looking as if she wanted to heal it.

Cole snorted and laid his sax on the bar. He reached over and grabbed the beer he'd started earlier. It hadn't dulled the fierce need that sliced into him every time he thought about her sweet lips opening up under his.

To hell with Kira Douglass. She could take her diamond eyes and soft lips and go heal someone else. What was wrong with him couldn't be fixed with a sweet kiss and an understanding look. Besides which, he had no desire to be healed. He needed the pain. Had intentionally blocked everything else out. Pain served as a constant reminder that he was alive. Whether he deserved to be or not.

Twin beams of light pierced the glass doors, illuminating the darkness inside the isolated houseboat. She was here. He downed the rest of the beer, tossed the bottle over the bar into the trash, and got up to return his sax to the worn leather case in his bedroom. He ran a quick gaze over the small room, pausing slightly at the large box he'd placed in the corner earlier that day. Calling himself a few choice names, he closed the folding door behind him. On his way to the deck, he absently kicked his old ratty deck shoes under the couch and tossed a magazine onto the shelf behind his reading chair.

It wasn't until he stepped outside that he realized he'd been cleaning up for her again. A scowl stole across his face. He leaned against the side railing and crossed his arms over his chest. For the hundredth time since she'd said her hasty good-byes last night, he asked himself why he hadn't kicked her off the boat the minute she'd confessed that P.J. was a dolphin, not a child.

He had no answer. Not one he'd admit to, anyway.

Well, he could correct that stupid mistake in about five minutes. And there would still be time to head to Key West for a set or two at Repo's.

"Cole?" Her soft voice floated to him through the humid night air.

He continued to lean on the railing as she climbed aboard. The moonlight gave her white slacks an almost neon brightness; the white stripes on her dark pullover also stood out. Her hair was pulled back in a loose ponytail. Wild strands of unruly curls blew gently around her face, making him wonder absently if she'd driven with the windows down. She looked . . . untamed. What had happened to his Sunday-school teacher?

She paused after she'd gotten her footing. He hadn't spoken to her yet, and some perverse notion kept him silent. She took a small step closer, and Cole realized he was testing her, anticipating what she would do next with something that much too closely resembled interest. He shifted slightly, crossing his ankles. She stopped.

He couldn't decide how that made him feel. He wanted to intimidate her, make her leave. He wanted her to fight back. He thought about the kiss they'd shared. Shared. He wanted to taste her lips again.

He abruptly pushed away from the railing and moved to the sliding glass door. "I'm going to get something to drink. Want anything?"

With his back to her, he had no idea how his somewhat rude welcome had gone over. He paused with his hand on the doorframe.

"If it wouldn't be too much trouble, a beer would be nice."

Her voice was low, her tone even. But he hadn't missed the underlying sarcasm. A private smile curved his lips. He didn't turn but merely nodded his head and went inside.

Stepping back onto the deck, he tucked one bottle under his arm and unscrewed the other, then wiped the damp glass off on his jeans and handed it to her. She had to walk a few steps to take it from him. From the silver sheen flashing in her moonlit eyes, the fact that he'd made her do so hadn't been lost on her.

Her fingers brushed his as she took the icy-cold bottle. He resisted the urge to pull his hand away, forcing himself to let the warmth of her skin register on his mind. Problem was, it also registered on his body. When she stood this close, he could smell the light citrus scent of her freshly washed hair. He should have known she would favor something sharp and tangy over soft and floral.

He struggled to recall his five-minute plan. Letting his hand drop, he busied himself flicking the cap off his beer. He knew he wasn't going to help her. Had P.J. been a child, he simply wouldn't have had a choice. But now . . .

He ignored the strange twinge near his heart. No. His decision to send her packing was the right one. If she stayed here, he'd have her in his bed. In his bed, underneath him, writhing. The very idea tempted him almost beyond his control; the image burned in his mind.

But he wasn't such a bastard that he'd seduce a woman who'd probably want more—and deserve more—from him than fleeting physical release.

And that was all he was capable of giving. All she'd get from him would be a good roll in the sack followed by a lot of pain. And he'd been the cause of far too much pain already.

Her soft sigh broke through his dark thoughts, and his body twitched in response. Her five minutes were up.

"About this fish thing," he began, tilting his head forward to look at her.

"Mammal," she corrected, her tone distracted.

Then, as if his voice had finally registered, her expression snapped into focus and onto him. She'd been a million miles away.

Without thinking, he leaned forward, allowing the moonlight to spill fully across her face. Her soft lips were bracketed by shallow grooves of concern. She was really worried about that damn fish.

He let loose a deep sigh. He'd like to think he was about to do her a favor. Only he knew better. Maybe he was more of a bastard than he'd thought. The idea depressed him. "Tell me who stole your fi—" He broke off, a slight smile curving his lips at her raised brow and narrow gaze. "Mammal. Who, Kira?"

The way he said her name gave Kira an inexplicable sense of security. A feeling she'd never thought to have around a man like Cole Sinclair. But she wasn't over the hump yet. When he heard who'd stolen P.J., she might very well find herself taking a quick hike back down the pier.

She looked him straight in the eye, knowing it was imperative that she speak with total conviction. "Juan Carlos Martinez."

Cole's eyes widened, and he sagged momentarily against the railing. Then he tipped his head back and laughed.

If she hadn't been so startled by the rich, full-bodied sound rumbling out of him, she would have been angry. "I take it you know who Martinez is?"

"If you mean do I know he's one of the most reclusive wealthy men to reside in the Keys, then the answer is yes. *My* question is do you have any idea just how Juan Carlos racked up all those zeros on his bank balance? Why he lives on his own key in virtual seclusion?"

"For the same reason you do, I imagine." Judging from the muscles clenching and unclenching his jaw, she'd surprised him with that one. She hurried to press her momentary advantage. "Men who run illegal contraband between the States and Cuba aren't usually comfortable in the spotlight, Mr. Sinclair. But then, I suspect you know that."

A slow smile crossed his face, but this time it held little humor. In fact, the gleam in his eyes gave her the distinct impression she'd just said the wrong thing.

He stepped away from the railing and she had to exert all her self-control not to flinch. He was at least half a foot taller than she, and his close stance forced her head back to maintain eye contact. It wasn't exactly a subtle form of intimidation, but it was very effective.

"Don't make judgments about things or people that you know nothing about. And don't believe everything you hear. As far as Juan Carlos is concerned, let's just say that if he does have your dolphin, then you might as well grab your nets and head out to sea to catch another one."

"No."

Cole shook his head, trying to hold his temper in check. This made two times in two days he'd had his control tested. Both of those occurrences were the fault of the woman standing in front of him. Question was, why did he let her get away with it? He forced his clenched muscles to relax. This was not his problem. She was not his concern.

"You have a death wish, sweet lips? That's fine by me. You go right ahead and try to steal your dolphin back. But count me out."

He leaned against the railing, crossing his arms in calculated nonchalance. The silence stretched out for several long minutes. He knew the instant she realized she'd lost. The tension in her jawline disappeared as her chin dipped in resignation. But what got to him was the brief flash of disappointment that had flickered through her diamond eyes. Not disappointment that she'd lost P.J. Disappointment in him.

And damn her, it jerked a tiny response from him.

"Well, it seems as if our business is concluded, then," she said softly. Any trace of what he'd seen in her eyes was gone, replaced by an irritating calm that shook his control more than her smart mouth ever had.

"Thank you for the beer, Mr. Sinclair."

She was two steps away before he acted. With a whispered oath he shoved off the railing. He raised a hand to stop her, but she halted when she heard the deck creak under his heavy weight. His hand dropped to his side, his fingers curling into a slowly tightening fist. Another long pause. "Don't go."

Her entire body stiffened. "What did you say?" Her voice was low, barely above a whisper.

Cole exhaled heavily. "Do you make things this hard on every man you meet? Or is it just me you take pleasure in tormenting?"

She turned then, her eyes wide with surprise and not a little aggravation. "*Me* torment *you*?" It was her turn to snort in disgust. "As far as I can tell, you're the one who's always in a foul mood." She jabbed a finger at his chest. "And don't you think if it were as simple as catching another dolphin, I'd have done that? Even if I could, capturing them is illegal unless you have a permit."

"But stealing a dolphin from one of the world's biggest crime bosses is okay?"

"Listen, mister, everything I've worked long and hard to achieve is on the line here. If I fail, it's not just me who suffers. You might think this is a lark, but I assure you the kids P.J. works with don't think so. If you'd come to the institute like I'd asked you to, you'd have seen that for yourself. Apparently, you had better things to do." She raised her hands as if to say she couldn't imagine what that could be.

Cole didn't much like her low opinion of him, which was strange since for the past couple of years he'd never cared what anyone thought about him. "I'm not a detective on a case, Ms. Douglass," he shot back, with emphasis on her name. "I don't work for you."

She swept a look of pure disdain over his onetime luxurious houseboat. "From the looks of things, you hardly work at all."

He grabbed her arms and tugged her until she came up hard against his chest. Pushing his face close to hers, he said, "For a woman who runs a school, you aren't very smart. You say I'm some low-life smuggler. If I was as low and amoral as you seem to believe—hell, maybe you even want me to be—then don't you think it would be wise not to rile me?" He pushed her away but kept his hold on her arms. "There's a whole bunch of empty swamp between you and anything resembling help out there. Now I'd suggest you close those pouty little lips and take that sweet fanny of yours and hightail it back to your car as fast as you can."

Kira's chest rose and fell in an effort to regain the breath that had been knocked out of her when he'd yanked her against him. The last time she'd been that close, he'd been kissing her. She wasn't sure which episode bothered her the most. She shouldn't have needed to be told to run and run fast. Common sense alone should have warned her she was taking a huge risk by goading him. But for a man who'd gone out of his way to keep her safe, even to the extent of taking on a bar full of bikers, he was working awfully hard to convince her she was in danger from him.

Or was he trying to convince himself?

She shook off that thought. She knew better than to assume he had any morals. His kiss had been the most amoral thing she'd ever experienced.

But the fact remained that she didn't think he'd hurt her. "If you think I'm in so much danger, then why did you ask me to stay a few minutes ago?"

He studied her much the same way she'd studied him earlier. "I'm not sure," he answered finally. The menace had disappeared from his voice, leaving a strange weariness that tugged at her despite the warnings to herself not to soften toward him. "But I imagine it's the same reason you didn't run away when you had the chance."

His eyes were so dark they held no light at all. Kira didn't mistake his meaning. "Is that the deal then? You'll help me if I . . . stay?"

He smiled. The shine of white teeth played off the bottomless black pools of his eyes, giving him an aura the other side of wicked. It was then Kira realized, deep down, that the reason she'd felt safe was because she truly hadn't believed all the rumors about his notorious past.

She did now. And still she stood there, waiting for his response with a rush of anticipation that had little to do with rescuing P.J. and a whole lot to do with finding out whether he intended to use his body to deliver the promise he was making with his smile.

"What exactly are you offering, Kira?"

Heat crept over her skin until her body felt as if it were on fire. She wished he'd stop staring at her like that. She wished he'd do something to put the fire out.

She should be angry with him for even insinuating she'd barter her body in return for his help. But it felt a bit hypocritical to deny the unsettling attraction that was simmering between them. Had been since she'd walked up to him in Repo's charming establishment. Still, that didn't mean she was ready to hit the sheets with him. For herself or P.J.

Did it?

She forced herself to maintain eye contact. "I won't deny there is . . . something happening." Her voice was even, but damnably husky. His smile broadened. "As unlikely as it seems," she added sharply.

Cole stepped toward her again, bringing them within a breath of contact. "Spell it out for me, Kira. Are you saying that if I help you, you'll go to bed with me?"

Kira had to tilt her head back to look at him, but she thrust her chin out a bit farther to let him know she wasn't intimidated by his frank conclusion. "If that's what it takes," she answered, her voice vibrating slightly. *Had she just said that?* She fought hard to convince herself it was purely self-sacrifice for P.J.'s sake.

Cole chuckled softly as he ran a callused finger along her jawline and around the curve of her chin. He pressed his fingertip gently into the soft indentation beneath her lips, parting them slightly. "You know as well as I do that I could have you in my bed—with or without a promise to help you."

Kira was stung, even as she grudgingly admitted the probable truth of his statement. But before she could shoot back, he lowered his head until his lips were almost touching hers.

His breath teased her lips with heat. "I'll help you, sweet lips," he said, his voice rough. "But not for sex."

FIVE

Kira had to work hard to keep her thoughts on track. "What then? What do you want?" As if it mattered, her mind jeered. And at that moment she wasn't too certain she would mind if he did want her in trade for his help.

He was going to kiss her. Every inch of her body knew it. She just wished he'd hurry up and do it.

"We can discuss that later." He brushed her lips with his in a manner that was more torture than kiss. "Much later."

His hand slid down to the side of her neck, and he gently pressed his fingers against her nape until her mouth fitted perfectly against his. The instant her lips parted, he deepened the contact. His lips pressed hard against hers as his tongue stole into her mouth, sampling her as if she were a fine and rare wine. The unexpectedly potent combination of the force of his lips and the gentle assault of his tongue sent Kira's surroundings spinning away. Her sole focus became his mouth on hers, the way he possessed her mouth, bonded with her in such an elemental way, she felt as if she'd carry his mark forever. Proudly.

She wanted to reach up to grip his shoulders, as much for the tactile need to feel the strength in him as for support, but her hands were trapped between them. He pulled her closer, wrapping his arms around her until she felt surrounded by a wall of muscled security. She should have felt threatened by his size and strength, but all she could think was that no one and nothing could reach her in the sanctity of his arms. It was a luxury she truly couldn't afford. She had to keep her head clear. P.J.'s—not to mention the institute's—future rested entirely on her. But it was so tempting, even for a minute or two, to let someone else help her carry the burden.

She started to pull away, but Cole tightened his hold on her. His kiss changed slightly, still dominant and possessive, but demanding in a different way. Almost as if he sought the same refuge in her arms as she sought in his. It was a foolish and dangerous notion, thinking he was vulnerable to her in even the slightest way. Even in her highly aroused state she knew she'd be a fool to fall for that again. Yet she sensed the desperation in his touch and was helpless in fighting the need to give back to him what he seemed so effortlessly to give to her.

She moved to change the kiss, to give instead of receive.

But Cole was having none of it. He seemed to be content to continue to make love to her mouth all night if she'd let him. Make love. Yes, Kira thought, for all the power and force behind his kiss, it was lovemaking.

With renewed determination she tried slowly to push his tongue with her own, silently asking permission to pleasure his mouth the way he'd pleasured hers. Abruptly he pulled his lips from hers, tucking her head against his chest and gently holding it there. She felt his hand move in slow strokes over her hair. For a while she simply stood in his arms, both of them breathing raggedly, hearts pounding.

Finally Cole leaned away and cupped the back of her head, tilting it gently back until her eyes met his. His gaze was dark, flat. His lips, swollen seductively from his heated assault, were the only outward sign that he'd felt any passion at all.

"We will spend time in bed together, Kira," he whispered, his voice raw, his expression fierce. "But because we both want to. Not as a payoff."

Kira wanted to tell him that he was wrong. The intensity behind the words and his expression made it clear he wanted her. But she knew better than to confuse want with need. She wished it were as simple as wanting him.

She suddenly felt more smothered than secure.

She desperately needed some air and time to think. Aware that she was no match for his strength, she still instinctively pushed against his chest. She sighed in relief when he dropped his arms. She devoutly ignored the flash of abandonment that accompanied it. Distance. She took several steps away from him, forcing herself to pull the salty night air slowly into her lungs. When she thought she could speak without that embarrassing huskiness, she turned to face him.

Cole had retreated to the opposite side of the small deck and was nursing his beer. It was as if he'd never touched her. When she spoke, he turned his full attention on her. Immediately, she felt his touch all over again. Would she ever get used to that penetrating black-eyed stare?

"If you're willing to help, then I think we'd better go over what I've learned so far." She strove to keep her tone neutral. But under his scrutiny, she was only marginally successful.

After a moment of tense silence he turned and placed his bottle back on the bench beside him, then looked back at her. She felt a momentary frisson race down her spine as it hit her that after all of this, he still might turn her down. Uneasily, she realized that her need for him to say yes went beyond her need to rescue P.J.

"I'm always willing, Kira," he said finally.

The breath she'd been holding puffed out in a

silent rush. It was difficult to ignore the effect those words had on her already overheated libido, but she doggedly pursued her original train of thought. "Is there somewhere we could sit down to talk? Inside maybe?"

Cole glanced through the sliding-glass doors into the darkened living room. "Too muggy. Why don't we go up top?"

Characteristically he simply stepped over to the ladder to the top deck and motioned for her to go up first. She hurried to the ladder before he could change his mind and quickly climbed to the top. Cole hoisted himself over the top rung a moment later.

The upper deck was railed in and consisted of the steering console and a padded bench. The canvas top that provided cover from the sun had been tacked down, leaving them bathed in moonlight. Cole tossed a couple of cushions down, silently motioning her to make herself comfortable opposite him.

Kira sat Indian fashion and rested her back lightly against the wall. Cole stretched his legs out in front of him, crossing them at the ankles. His feet rested against the edge of her cushion. Kira fought the urge to let her gaze drift from his bare feet up along his denim-clad legs. Instead, she shifted slightly and looked out over the moonlit water.

Cole remained silent, apparently waiting for her to begin. Kira felt at once calm and flustered. The air was warm and the moon bright, but Cole's mere presence made the peaceful surroundings seem fraught with tension. But it was an addictive, intimate sort of tension that she almost enjoyed.

"After P.J. was discovered missing," she began, "I questioned all of my employees. We have eight. We also occasionally have college students conducting various studies at the institute, but none at the moment. The only other people with access to Dr. Dolphin are the various physicians and therapists who use the facilities for their patients."

She paused, glancing quickly at Cole when he didn't respond. He was staring at her intently, but he remained silent. She shifted her gaze back to the black water. "My staff isn't paid very much." Remembering his earlier jab, she darted a quick look at him. He inclined his head slightly, and she knew her point had been taken and smiled with satisfaction. She turned her attention back to the water. "Most of them have been with me from the beginning and are supremely dedicated to the dolphins. I know it couldn't have been one of them."

"I wouldn't rule that out."

She whipped her head around. "Why do you say that? You don't even know them."

"You're too defensive about it. I think you're wondering if one of them *did* do it."

Kira couldn't fault his logic, but it was unnerving to think he could read her so easily. "Maybe so. But only because after checking everything out thoroughly, I'm convinced that Mr. Martinez had to have help to steal P.J."

"And it has to be someone who knows the dolphins and is intimately familiar with Dr. Dolphin's daily routines."

"Yes, but that still doesn't prove it's one of my people." She eyed him again warily. He was very sharp. She was suddenly curious to know just what the truth was behind the rumors that floated around about his smuggling past.

But now was not the time to ask him personal questions. Besides, she'd come to him precisely because of his shady background.

"You still haven't told me how you discovered it was Martinez who stole your dolphin."

His challenging tone made it clear he had his doubts about her theory. "Actually, I found out accidentally." She shifted so her back rested squarely against the wall and pulled her knees up to her chest. Wrapping her arms around them, she looked directly at Cole as she spoke, knowing it was crucial he believe her. "The only way P.J. could get out on his own would be the underwater gate that separates the lagoon from the canal. The canal then empties out into the Gulf."

"Was the gate damaged at all?" Cole asked abruptly.

"No, there's been no damage to the gate or the fence. But I'd already ascertained that none of my employees had accidentally opened the gate, so the only other possibility was that he'd been taken. Stolen."

"And of course the first person who came to mind was an international crime lord."

Kira frowned at Cole's sarcastic response but didn't let him bait her into a sharp retort. Even she realized how fantastical it seemed. "Of course not. I set up a meeting with all my employees to discuss how we would handle P.J.'s disappearance with the media and the adjustments that we'd have to make for the upcoming investors' presentation. At the time I wasn't sure exactly how he'd disappeared. Actually it took a while to really comprehend that he had. The whole idea of someone taking him was so bizarre that I wanted to believe there was some simple explanation. So I didn't call the police."

Cole snorted in obvious disgust.

Aggravated by his condescending attitude, Kira heatedly defended her decision. "If I reported a stolen dolphin to the police, it would have become a matter of public record. As I said before, P.J. has been the subject of numerous documentaries focusing on his ability to work with handicapped children. Those tapes are a large part of my presentation to gain the interest of potential investors. If word got out that P.J. was missing, I was afraid some of the investors would back out. To call them a skeptical group would be an understatement. So I thought it was best to keep it quiet until we'd had time to do some investigating of our own."

Her tone all but dared him to comment. He lifted his bare shoulders in a shrug that said her reasons didn't concern him, since it was too late to change what she'd done. Kira swallowed her anger and forced herself to relax. She wondered what would penetrate his seeming indifference. She smiled tentatively and pushed on with her story. "We went on to discuss the meeting, and as everyone talked about which investors seemed the most likely to drop out, the same name kept coming up. KeyMar Industries."

Cole sat up a bit straighter. "One of Martinez's front companies for dumping cash."

Kira didn't even bother wondering how he knew that. In fact, it would be a real boon to her if he had inside information on Martinez. "I didn't know that at the time. All I knew was that spokespersons for this company had called several times, each time questioning a different employee at length about a number of things related to our institute. Each thought nothing of it, but when we all sat down together, it became clear that the sum of information they'd requested was more than the standard-type questions potential investors ask."

"I agree it sounds suspicious, but I don't see why Martinez or any other investor would want to steal a dolphin."

"Neither did I." Kira's voice became stronger.

"But it just seemed too coincidental. KeyMar had made inquiries at least twice a week for the last several weeks, but they haven't called once since P.J.'s disappearance. It might have been a coincidence, but it was all I had to go on."

"Why didn't you call the police in then? Juan Carlos Martinez isn't the sort of man you play amateur detective with."

"I know." Kira's voice hardened as she thought of P.J. being held by a man reputed to have no conscience and even fewer morals. She forced her words past the lump forming in her throat. "I started to, but then I realized that I'd have to tell them who had him. I figured as part of their investigation they'd naturally have to question him. Considering the questions his people asked, I figured he might have taken P.J. specifically because this dolphin works best with autistic kids. But if Martinez thought he was under suspicion, he could just as easily steal another one and—" She broke off, unable to put her worst fears into words.

"You're right, Kira," Cole said quietly. "If Martinez does have him and even suspects you know he's responsible, he'll destroy P.J. without a second thought."

Kira flinched at the dead certainty in Cole's voice. It was the nightmare she'd been living with every minute of every day and every night since P.J.'s disappearance. And it was the real reason she didn't want the police involved. Even if she lost the institute, she'd never forgive herself for putting P.J. at such risk if there was another way.

Something about his tone penetrated through the horrifying thought of possibly losing such a valued mammal and companion. "You seem to know a lot about Martinez." She paused for a second, unsure of how to phrase the rest of the question without risking being tossed overboard. She didn't have to worry. As usual, Cole was one step ahead of her.

"Is that why you chose me, Kira?" His voice was soft but contained a thread of steel. "Do you think I worked for Martinez?"

Kira knew the next words she spoke would likely seal P.J.'s fate. She swallowed and moistened her lips. "I never really thought it out that far. I figured anyone in a . . . line of work such as yours would know about him. Yours was the only name I'd heard in connection with that type of, uh, lifestyle." She studied him closely, but he was very good at concealing his thoughts, and she had no idea how he felt about her explanation. Nervously, she added, "The main reason I tracked you down was because you helped Toby Jantzen."

"A smuggler with a heart of gold, is that it?"

Kira winced at the amused cynicism in his voice. And she'd imagined him to have some deep vulnerability. How stupid and totally like her to try to romanticize him so she wouldn't feel so afraid. Her cheeks burned in humiliation. She'd been a complete fool. Cole Sinclair was hard all the way through.

P.J. was as good as dead.

"What did you do next?"

Kira had been so certain his next words would be good-bye that his question took her totally by surprise. "I didn't tell my staff what I'd learned. I figured I'd try to dig up more information first, make certain I was right. I started asking questions and quietly looking up any information I could find on KeyMar. It didn't take long to find out Martinez owned it. After that I started to wonder why a man like Martinez would want P.J."

"Which brings us back to my first question."

"I talked to each of my employees again, individually this time. I tried to find out exactly what each of them had been asked and had revealed."

"Quite the little detective. Maybe you're in the wrong line of work." Cole shook his head.

It was obvious he had no respect for what she'd accomplished on her own. If anything, he thought she was an idiot for taking the risk. She smiled and pretended that she thought he was really amused by her actions. "Well, I confess to being an armchair detective. But in this case, I just tried to imagine why I would want a trained dolphin bad enough to steal one."

"Okay, Ms. V. I. Warshawski, what did you come up with?"

Kira's smile was real this time. So he was a Paretsky fan too. She thought about all those books on the shelf below and wondered how many were mysteries. "A lot of the questions had to do with how the dolphins helped the kids with learning disabilities, specifically autism."

"Considering the type of school you run, that doesn't seem so odd."

"It wouldn't be, but combined with the other questions about the dolphins' schedule and daily routine, I began to wonder. It seemed as if the caller made certain not to ask any one person enough to make him or her suspicious, and each call dealt with one topic at a time."

"Do your employees make a habit of divulging that sort of information to anyone who calls?" His tone made it clear he thought she might as well have handed the thief a key to the front door.

"Yes. Cole, it's not like we're guarding state secrets here. We rely completely on investors to keep our doors open. My employees are encouraged to be as helpful as possible and answer any questions they can in order to encourage the investors' enthusiasm. It isn't unusual for people to become very interested and devoted to the dolphins. They are really incredible creatures. Our main concern is usually keeping an overeager tourist or individual from accidentally harming a dolphin out of misguided enthusiasm or ignorance."

The moonlight did little to reveal if she'd swayed his opinion. Whatever was going on behind those enigmatic black eyes of his remained a secret.

Kira purposely stopped her story for a moment. She felt she'd been cramming this information down his throat and wanted to give him time to assimilate it.

Again, she'd underestimated him.

"So I take it Martinez has a kid with autism, and he snatched the dolphin as a means to cure him?"

Kira's eyes widened. He'd been paying closer attention than she'd thought. He must have made one hell of a smuggler. Only when his gaze jerked to hers did she realize she'd spoken that last part out loud.

"What I mean," she rushed on before he got angry, "is that it took me a while to figure that out. I talked to every therapist and doctor I could find, trying to find out if Martinez had ever brought a child in for an examination or treatment."

"Did he?"

"No. At least not that I could find."

Cole let out what sounded like a sigh of irritation. He tunneled his fingers through his hair, then linked them behind his head. His relaxed pose didn't for a second hide the tension that radiated down the length of his body. "So how did you find out? Knock on his door and ask?"

"No, of course not. I wouldn't take that kind of risk."

Cole raised an eyebrow, his expression saying better than ten well-aimed comebacks what he thought of her ability to discern danger.

She tamped down her anger. Damn the man for putting her on the defensive. "Because of the type of investor we attract, I'm invited to a fair number of social functions. I don't always attend." She didn't add that invariably she felt like a sideshow act, invited only because of her connection to the dolphins that everyone seemed so intrigued about. Ever aware she could be cultivating another much-needed investor, she always answered the endless queries enthusiastically, which wasn't difficult since the subject never tired her. But being more at home in the lagoon with the dolphins than rubbing elbows with the rich, she found it difficult to endure the endless inane gossip and industry-insider talk.

For once, however, the invitation to a swank event had been eagerly received. She leaned forward and folded her arms atop her knees as she related the events of the evening to Cole. "I was invited to a party held by one of my investors out on Ramrod Key. Since I'd learned Martinez owned one of the small cays off Ramrod, I went in hopes of subtly questioning any possible acquaintance of his for information."

"I take it you were successful?"

Kira smiled as she recalled how it had happened. "Actually, it was ridiculously easy. I had worked up this long list of every imaginable innocent question I could ask, afraid I'd blow it by asking the wrong person the wrong thing. In the end I happened to be using the ladies' room at the same time as two of Mrs. Martinez's bridge pals. They were discussing the difficulty the Martinezes were having keeping housemaids, and apparently thinking they were alone, one of the ladies made a nasty remark about how they might have better luck hiring a zoo keeper."

Kira's tone turned progressively more bitter as she went on. "The other one responded that she thought it was simply a rumor about Carlos having a son who was so demented he kept him locked up like an animal." Kira looked up at Cole, unable to hide the anguish and fierce anger in her expression. "The first woman seemed to think otherwise, but then someone else came in and they left."

Without thinking, she put her hand on Cole's thigh. She was so angry over the injustice being done to a child, she hardly noticed the way Cole's entire leg went rigid under her touch. "Don't you see? It all makes sense. The questions about how dolphins help autistic children. Martinez having a son in a locked room. Cole, a man like Martinez, a Cuban who practically invented the term 'machismo,' would rather steal P.J. in hopes of a miracle cure for his son than admit to the world—or himself—that he'd sired a defective child. His heir."

Cole stared into her glittering eyes for a long moment. Despite his repeated attempts to prevent it, he was totally captivated by her. She was so certain of the truth of her story that she was short of breath. Her intensity brought on a violent rush of memories he'd kept locked away for two long years. Kira reminded him of Felicia. Felicia had had the same fierce loyalty for anyone under her protection. It had ultimately caused her death. And if Kira wasn't careful, it would cause her death too. The mere thought of Kira being in mortal danger made his body tighten painfully for a minute; then he shoved the entire episode from his mind.

Ruthlessly, he turned his attention to what he'd convinced himself was his real attraction to Kira Douglass. He purposely let his gaze shift lower. He watched with a forced sense of detached fascination as her breasts rose and fell in her effort to regain her breath. Feeling himself begin to harden in response to her agitated and excited state, he gave himself over to it. This response he understood. This feeling he could accept from her. Sexual desire. A hot, primal, animalistic, purely male response. He wanted to revel in the safety of it.

Then his gaze drifted lower and collided with her hand clutching his knee.

She seemed to be unaware of the action, but his

gaze brought it to her attention. She followed his eyes downward, and as soon as she realized she was touching him, she pulled her hands away. "I . . . I'm sorry," she said hesitantly.

Cole looked up again and became trapped in her eyes. "Why?"

The moonlight cast her face in shades of white and gray, but he swore he could feel the flush that rose to her cheeks. Still, he remained silent. Despite the voice in his head yelling at him to retract the question, telling him to just yank her onto his lap and get on with it, he wanted to know what she would say. He was daring her to put into words the one subject he'd rather die than discuss.

"I know you'd rather I not touch you."

Cole had to resist the urge to grab her, to beg her to touch him anywhere she damn well pleased, and quickly. Her voice was so damn soft and honest. Her lips were made to be cherished. It took every last ounce of restraint he had to force his mind off of that carnal path.

He'd gotten his answer. He tucked his hands deeper under his crossed arms, clenching them into tight fists against the raging desire to touch her, knowing that if he so much as lifted his hand, he'd have her naked and under him before he could breathe her name.

Kira wasn't one to back away from a subject just because it might prove difficult, but he refused to pursue the topic any further. "I can't help you if you refuse to face the fact that one of your staff members is probably in on this. You've got to be prepared. Do you understand?"

"Yes."

One word. How did she pack so much hope into one simple word? Cole felt a sudden desperate urge to order her off his boat, out of his life. Kira was a threat to him on every level. With every word she spoke, every innocent movement of her body, he wanted her more. She was forcing him to see just how deep his deception went within himself. He'd actually convinced himself he could help her out and then take her to bed and that would be the end of that. Even when he'd begun to realize he might have to keep her in his bed for a while before he got his fill of her, he'd told himself he could handle it.

He looked into her eyes and understood those assurances for what they were. Lies. A desperate attempt to convince himself he deserved even a fleeting moment of pleasure. Damn her for giving him that hope.

A woman like Kira, who cared for the hurt and disabled and vulnerable of the world, had sensed the void in him where his soul once resided. And he doubted she'd let him go until she'd tried every damn thing she could think of to give it back to him.

But his soul couldn't be given back. He'd sold it. Bartered it away years ago for a life of lies and deceit. And if he'd ever needed proof of just how unredeemable he was, Kira had just handed it to him engraved in shattered diamonds.

Because he was damned if he could stop wanting her even when he knew his wanting would likely destroy them both.

"Give me two days, then meet me back here," he said roughly, pushing himself to his feet in one fluid motion. She rocked back on her heels, and without another word he turned to lower himself down the stairs.

Kira stood up, caught off guard by his sudden move. He was halfway down the ladder before she gathered her wits enough to form a coherent question. She leaned over the short wall in time to see him drop to the deck below. "What are you going to do?"

He looked up at her, his expression unreadable. "Right now? I'm going to go swimming."

"Swimming?" Kira shouted. She didn't wait for a reply. She swung quickly down the ladder and found herself alone. She hadn't heard a splash, so Cole was on the boat somewhere. "Cole!" she shrieked, not caring how she sounded. She'd just poured out her heart to the man, and all he could do was issue an order, then blithely announce he was in the mood for a moonlight dip? Not while she was still breathing air.

She started to head inside but heard a muffled

thump from the rear of the boat. Without another thought she hopped onto the narrow ledge that ran along the outside length of the main cabin and tip-toed carefully to other end. She had no intention of falling in. Given his arrogance, Cole would probably assume she'd elected to join him.

Her mind rapidly sorted through the myriad things she wanted to say to him. As she neared the back she was fully prepared to tell him exactly what he could do with his curt orders and assumption of her obedience. She hopped down to the back deck, mouth open, ready to let go with both barrels, but not a sound passed her lips.

In front of her, in his full God-given glory, was a very healthy-looking, utterly naked Cole Sinclair. He was facing the water and had just propped one foot on the side railing as if to launch himself over the side. If he knew he had an audience, he didn't let on.

She had to say something to make him stop. She was primed for an argument and desperately wanted to say her piece. But her brain just wasn't sending the proper signals to her mouth. It was much too busy processing every little, and not so little, detail of Cole's incredible physique. It didn't temper her anger any when she realized that she was a tad dis-appointed that she was only being treated to a rear view. As it occurred to her that by saying something she might get his attention as well as a peek at the rest of him, she opened her mouth, but at that very moment he dove over the side and disappeared beneath the silvery black surface of the cove.

She raced to the edge, waiting for him to surface. After a long moment his head and upper torso shot up at least a hundred yards out. His hair was so dark against the even darker water that if it hadn't been for the full moon, she'd never have spotted him. "Cole!"

He'd been looking in her direction and didn't move when she called his name. He had known she was there, the jerk.

Bracing her arms on the side railing, she leaned as far over the side as she could. "I wasn't finished talking to you yet," she called across the moonlit water. "Do you think you might put off your swim for a few more minutes while we clear away the remaining details?"

"No," he called back. "Why don't you drop your clothes and dive in?"

SIX

Kira's mouth dropped open. Of all the . . . His tone seemed sincere, but she could picture his cynically amused expression, and her blood boiled. She pressed her lips together, trying to keep from shooting her mouth off. He was trying to bait her, and she wasn't about to fall for it. No way would she let him lure her into the water with him, clothed or not. It didn't help matters that she couldn't erase the image of his "bait." She cleared her throat. "No, thank you. I spend too much time in the water as it is. I don't suppose you'd tell me what you're planning on doing in the next forty-eight hours?"

"Depends on where you are and what we're doing when you ask," he shot back.

Despite attempts not to, Kira had to restrain the urge to smile. Cole had made blatant suggestions to her before—had all but announced he planned to get her into his bed. But he'd never teased her in quite this way. He was almost being . . . friendly.

Maybe she did need some exercise. Her brain was obviously fogging up again. Cole Sinclair, friendly? Not likely.

"Fine," she called back. "I'll give you the two days. But I'm not coming out here again." She didn't dare pause. "You meet me at the institute. I think it's time you got up close and personal with the other dolphins. I should be done around six."

She turned and ducked into the main cabin. She knew if she catwalked back along the side, it would give him the opportunity to respond, or worse, given his obvious superb physical condition, swim back to the boat before she could get to the pier. She slipped out onto the back deck and jumped up onto the pier, then crossing her fingers for a smooth getaway and digging her keys out of her pants pocket, she hopped in her car.

"Damn," Cole muttered. He watched the headlights on Kira's car shoot white beams across the cove in front of him, then turn and become swallowed up by the night. "Damn."

How had she so neatly outmaneuvered him? He'd thought his spur-of-the-moment idea for a swim was pretty ingenious at the time. Watching Kira's expressive face and listening to her heartfelt description had started an ache in the vicinity of his chest. It was either dive overboard and take a cooling dip or yank her onto his lap. He'd chosen swimming because he doubted seriously she'd have stayed in his lap for long. And when they made love, it wasn't going to be on the rough indoor-outdoor carpeting of the upper deck.

Cole started to pull himself across the cove with long, lazy strokes. He forced his mind to the conversation that had preceded her abrupt departure and away from all thoughts of bedding Kira Douglass. For now.

He'd known she was behind him on the boat just before he'd dived in. That she hadn't simply taken him at his word and left surprised him, although he didn't know why. She'd never taken his word for anything yet—why should this time have been any different?

He took a deep breath and began swimming faster with short, pounding strokes. After ten solid minutes he dove under, then burst up through the surface, expending a final surge of energy. Exhausting himself in the water wasn't helping. He couldn't ignore the fact that he hadn't exactly been irritated by her refusal to be pushed around. As a matter of fact, he'd been tempted to turn and face her on the back deck. Only he knew damn well they'd end up doing the exact thing he'd been trying to avoid when he'd stripped in the first place. The very idea of her studying his naked body had aroused him so intensely, he'd been completely thrown off by it. In the end he'd simply gone over the side. Any hope that she'd either been embarrassed or irritated into leaving had been quickly dashed when she'd called his name out into the night.

Cole reached up and gripped the railing on the side of the boat with both hands. But instead of pulling himself on board, he hung there for several long minutes, willing the water to quell the arousal that was still raging even after his strenuous workout. Giving up, he swore softly and hauled himself over the edge.

"Damn," he muttered again as he traipsed into his bedroom moments later, heedlessly dripping water all over the floor. He glanced at the large box in the corner, then heaved a sigh as he tilted his head back, rotating shoulder muscles still stiff with tension no amount of exercise would ease. He grabbed a T-shirt off his bed and used it to towel himself off, then tossed it on the floor behind him and climbed into bed. After punching his pillow several times, he gave up and flopped over on his back. Even the cool feel of the white percale beneath his back and the clingy black satin draped across his chest did little to soothe him or entice sleep.

He muttered an oath, then several more, then let a whole string loose. But even that tried-and-true form of stress reduction did little to ease the strange tension that had invaded his mind and body. With a last earthy curse he pillowed his head on his arms and stared up at the ceiling. He let his mind drift and gradually fell asleep with visions of shattered diamonds playing at the edges of his mind.

"Felicia! *No!*" Cole shot forward, adrenaline pumping hard through his body, his heart pounding so rapidly, he knew it would burst. Fear, horror, then agonizing pain sliced through him like a razor-sharp sword. *Dear God, what have I done?* "No! Damn you, Marcos!" They were too far away; he couldn't get there. No matter how fast he swam, it was too late. Dead. All dead. How many of them had there been? He watched helplessly as the small bodies blown into the air by the vicious explosion rained down around him in scattered, indistinguishable parts. "No . . . sweet Lord, no," he sobbed.

It wasn't until he tried to swim to them and became hopelessly tangled that he realized he was sitting upright in his own bed. Awake.

"Damn!" he shouted, willing his heart to slow down and the ghastly images to fade from his mind. When he thought he was under control, he ripped off the sweat-soaked sheet tangled around legs that had been treading water in his dream. Climbing out of bed, he moved into the small bathroom and splashed cold water over his face and chest. Not bothering to dry himself, he stepped back into the bedroom. One look at the mangled remains of his bedclothes kept him moving until he sat on the rear deck.

Even the balmy midnight air felt good against his overheated naked skin. Raking his fingers through his hair, Cole let his head drop forward to rest in his palms, his elbows on his knees. He should never have gone to bed before dawn.

A rough sound of disgust echoed across the cove. Stupid, stupid. He hadn't had the nightmare in months. And going to sleep at night had not been the only reason for its return. The other was a certain brunette with eyes and lips that plucked at the soul he wasn't sure he had.

"Damn her," Cole muttered, even as he admitted it was his own fault.

His first instinct was to leave a note for old Sandy, letting him know he'd need another security guard for his pier—although it was his opinion, one he'd shared many times with the grizzled conch, that no one would bother with anything out here anyway. He shook his head at the fanciful idea that he could escape his demons by running. If there'd been any chance at that, he'd have left the Keys two years ago.

He knew better. He would face them and live with them every day until he died. The best he could do was make it as bearable as possible.

Besides which, the only thing of value he had left was his word. And he had given it to Sandy.

And Repo. And to his lasting regret, he'd also given it to Kira Douglass. Not in so many words, but in his own mind the commitment was made. If he went back on his word, he was left with nothing. Nothing to separate him from the human beings he had spent almost a decade of his life trying to bring to justice. Nothing to prove to the only ones he had cared about that their lives weren't lost because he had lost all human emotion.

A familiar ache clenched inside his chest, and Cole knew that for this night, he would be unable to keep the demons away. But before he allowed himself to replay all the violence and horror once again, he forced his mind back for just a moment to those diamondlike eyes and warm, caring smile. If she was partly at fault for lowering the walls, she could help prepare him to deal with the consequences.

Several hours later, exhausted emotionally, Cole watched a glorious sun break over the horizon and thought about what he had to do in the next two days. The contacts he was going to reestablish. He thought of the man who'd been trying to lure him back for over a year. Reese would be thrilled. And all for a damn fish. A vision of Kira telling him about a boy locked in a room, entreaty pouring from her eyes and lips, flashed in his mind. He let his head drop to his hands once again. "Jesus, Sinclair," he muttered. "What have you gotten yourself into this time?"

❖————————❖

Kira ripped the apron off and threw it into the corner of her office with a succinct oath. Rio's appetite wasn't improving, and she was finding it almost impossible to hide the strain she was under from her employees. "Dammit, Cole, where the hell are you?" she asked her empty office as she quickly stripped off her shorts and bathing suit. He'd said two days, and she'd given them to him. Not that she had any real choice. She glanced at the clock. Eight. The rest of the staff had left hours ago. *Where was he?*

She hadn't realized just how heavily she'd been counting on him. But as six o'clock had come and gone, her mood had slowly shifted from forced optimism to anger. Now she just felt stupid. What had gotten into her, anyway? She snorted in disgust as Cole's naked backside flashed across her mind for the millionth time. She'd let her own bruised ego get in the way of P.J.'s best interests. If anything happened to him . . .

She was startled out of her thoughts by a knock on her office door. *He had come after all!* She hastily pulled on and tucked in her tank top and zipped up her clean pair of white shorts. As she reached for the knob with one hand, she quickly ran her hand through her hair with the other. She aborted the move just as she pulled the door open. "Well, it's about ti—" She broke off midword as she saw who stood outside her door. "Paul? I thought you left hours ago." She knew he had, but was too startled to say anything else.

His expression changed from its initial curiosity over her greeting to a sheepish smile. "Yeah, I did. I went out with some friends, and we decided to take Frank's boat over to one of the deserted keys to party. When I went home to change, I realized I'd lost my house key and figured it must have dropped here. I saw the light under your door and decided to pop in so you wouldn't hear me and be alarmed."

His explanation was entirely plausible, so why wasn't she buying it? He seemed nervous. Plastering what she hoped was a casual smile on her face, she said, "I'll help you look. Are your friends waiting?" As she spoke she left her office, locking the door as she slipped out, though for the life of her she didn't know why. There was nothing of any importance in her office except client files. She mentally shrugged and walked quickly to the main reception area.

Kira tossed a glance over her shoulder to make sure Paul was right behind her. He was. She couldn't read anything unusual in his expression, but the chill trickling down her spine kept her alert. "Where do you think you dropped them?" she asked once she reached the main desk.

"I looked in here already," he answered, his glance averted as he apparently scanned the room again.

"Let's go back and check the lockers." They went around the desk and into the small room that housed the lockers used by the employees. Paul pulled his open, and a pile of junk literally fell into Kira's arms. On top was a crumpled piece of neon-green paper. Without thinking, she shoved the load in her arms into the empty locker next to Paul's and snagged the green wad of paper off the top.

"Have you seen this iguana?" she read out loud from the bold copy slashed across the brightly colored page. There was a grainy black-and-white, or actually, black-and-lime-green photo of a narrow-eyed man holding a large iguana. She choked back the simultaneous urge to laugh and gag. Even if Iggy hadn't been in the picture, she'd have recognized that iguana anywhere. It was Elvis. Trying for a steady voice, she continued, "Large reward for any information that leads to reuniting me with my companion, Elvis."

Paul groaned and rolled his eyes. "Just when you think you've seen it all." He reached out and took the flier from her hands, crumpled it up into a ball, and tossed it back in his locker. "I went down to a club in the lower keys last night and found this thing on my windshield when I left. Can you believe it? Next thing you know, we'll have a wave of Elvis sightings."

Kira blanched at the thought and quickly buried her head in one of the lockers beside Paul's. What had Cole done with the beast anyway? She knew she should be ashamed for not even thinking to ask him about it. But she figured with all that had been happening lately, she was excused.

"Bingo!"

Kira looked up in time to see Paul extract a silver key attached to a leather thong from the bowels of his locker. "Good. I hope this hasn't ruined your evening," she added, leaning against the locker door to close it, hoping he'd take off quickly.

"They'll wait for me."

"Don't tell me, you have the keg," she said, trying for a teasing tone.

"Nah, I'm the only one who can navigate Frank's boat around the reefs in the dark."

Kira stilled and tried to keep her face carefully blank. "I see." She didn't meet Paul's eyes in the sudden quiet that filled the small room.

After a second that stretched out painfully long, Paul began to shove everything back into his locker, mumbling something about promising to clean his locker soon.

Kira intervened. "I'll do this, go on. Wouldn't want to risk them leaving and running aground somewhere."

Paul laughed with a bit more force than she thought her comment warranted. "Never happen. Listen, thanks for the help. I'll, uh, see you on Monday."

Kira pasted on a smile and waved good-bye. She stood for a moment after he left, wondering if she'd read too much into their conversation. Her gaze fell on the crumpled green sheet. She snatched it up, folded it, and shoved it into her pocket. She quickly slammed the door to keep all the junk from tumbling back out and hurried back to her office. It wasn't until she got to her office door that she realized she'd locked her keys inside.

"Hell," she muttered. "I'll never make a good spy."

"Not if you don't keep your voice down."

Kira screamed and jumped a foot in the air. When she regained half a breath, she turned to find Cole leaning negligently against the wall in the shadowy hallway. "You scared the stuffing out of me."

"That's why they hired me as a spy, and not you."

Her anger fled as a frown flashed across his face. She hadn't missed his use of the word "they," and apparently neither had he. A million questions were stalled on the tip of her tongue, begging to be asked. But with miraculous fortitude, she ignored them. Given the fierce scowl shadowing his features, it was a sure bet he wouldn't have answered her anyway.

"What took you so long?" she asked. "I was beginning to think you weren't coming."

"Contrary to what you apparently think, I do have other commitments. You aren't paying me for round-the-clock obedience."

"I wasn't aware that was a commodity that could be bought from you," she shot back. Was it impossible to be near him without being constantly on the defensive? "Besides which," she continued, a phony smile curving her lips, "as far as I know, we haven't agreed I'm paying you at all. Have you decided on a price? And if so, how much extra does it run for the obedience?"

The return of the nightmare two nights before had convinced Cole as nothing else could that, no matter the cost, he would not—could not—afford to react to Kira Douglass again. Yet one smart-ass response delivered through those wickedly curved lips, and he felt his carefully reconstructed walls shake as if they'd been made of papier-mâché. He did manage to restrain the urge to smile.

He turned and strolled back down the hallway, forcing her to hurry if she wanted to keep up. That would get her mind off of what services she could purchase and back on the defensive. Just where he wanted her.

"Wait a minute. Come back here."

Damn her. Was it too much to ask that she get offended predictably? But the smile surfaced anyway, safely hidden as his back was to her. He had every intention of stopping, but he walked a few more steps anyway. It wouldn't do to give her even the slightest upper hand.

"Any chance I could make a one-time payment for some breaking and entering?" she called out to him, apparently unaffected by his attempts to goad her. "Of course, I can only pay on delivery, since my purse is in my office on the other side of this locked door."

It wasn't any use. He'd lost the battle before it had begun. Cole wiped the smile from his face, surprised at his reluctance to do so, then faced her. She was lounging casually against her office door, one trim ankle crossed over the other. He felt the heat center in his body. The scowl formed naturally. "Stop it, dammit!" he wanted to yell at her, shocked at how close he came to actually doing so.

What was happening to him? He should never have let her get to him. He didn't want this, didn't need it. But apparently his mind and his body weren't in total agreement on just what his needs and wants were. Bedding her and befriending her were on opposing sides as far as he was concerned. And it was rapidly becoming apparent that the trick was going to be finding a way to get one without committing himself to the other.

He let his gaze rake insolently up her tanned and nicely toned legs to rest on the formfitting tank top that molded her equally nicely toned upper body.

And he intended to bed her.

He had to give her credit, her posture tensed as he drew closer, but she didn't flinch or change positions. He wasted several seconds wondering what she'd do if he walked right up until his body was flush with hers and kissed her. Some small piece of sanity stopped him a few inches shy of that goal.

"I don't suppose you have a hairpin or credit card on you?"

Kira's eyes widened, and Cole had to glance down at the door to keep from smiling.

"How good a smuggler were you, anyway? Didn't they train you to do this sort of stuff a bit more . . . I don't know. Never mind."

"Well, it seems I left home without my tools," he responded sardonically. "I could have you inside in two seconds flat with nothing, but I didn't think you'd appreciate having to repair the door."

She stood there silently, staring at him, and Cole cursed the questions he saw in her eyes. He had absolutely no intention of explaining his past to her or anyone else. She'd come to him; it was *his* trust that needed to be earned here. Still, a few carefully chosen words just might scare her enough to send those questions sailing from her mind.

He turned and rested a shoulder on the door. A few inches to the left, and she'd be nestled under the crook of his arm. He bent down slowly, not stopping when she shifted her gaze to focus on the hallway in front of her. When he was a breath away from her ear, he whispered, "Sorry if I failed some test, but breaking and entering wasn't part of my job description." He waited several tense seconds, willing her to take the bait.

"What exactly was your job description?"

"You really want to know?" Damn, what was he trying to do? Give her another chance to say no? No, this was for the best. Before she could respond, he said, "Gunrunner."

He'd expected at least a trace of fear, maybe some revulsion, or at the very least, moral indignation. Instead, her eyes rounded, and she actually leaned closer to him. Maybe danger was a turn-on for her? Somehow he doubted it.

"And you can't pick a simple lock?"

Cole felt the ludicrous urge to defend his former profession. Well, the part he'd told her about, anyway. Instead, he did what he did best. He let his actions speak for him. He turned his body toward her, forcing her to shift until she was between him and the door. He placed one palm on the doorframe slightly above her head and brought the other up between them. He made no effort to keep his hand from brushing casually across her breasts as he raised it up to her face. He combed a few windblown strands away from her forehead, silently locking her gaze with his. Then he let his fingertips drift along the plane of her cheek, down the curve of her chin, to rest lightly on the side of her neck. He watched as her pupils slowly expanded, edging over the tiny fractured light of her eyes, pressing his fingers a bit harder against the side of her neck as her pulse picked up speed.

He'd meant to stay detached, to trap her in his gaze and then calmly inform her that with the right pressure, he could kill her instantly. But a soft, warm breath escaped her lips when he pressed his fingers against her pulse, and the last thing on his mind was scaring her. He wanted to stroke her, tease her, seduce her into giving some of that life force to him.

And what he saw in her eyes told him he could have what he was so desperately beginning to crave.

With the last shred of control he had, he forced himself to recall the actions he had set into motion less than twenty-four hours ago. Actions that precluded fogging his mind with passionate images, much less allowing his body to be depleted with an intense sexual encounter. And "intense" was a mild term for the explosion he expected to take place when he finally pushed himself into her body. No. It might very well be the last pleasure he allowed himself, and if he was to be damned for it, then it would be perfection or nothing.

As casually as he could, he slid his finger from her throat to her shoulder, then drew it halfway down her arm. He got sidetracked tracing a lazy pattern on the soft underside of her elbow, but when he realized his mind was drifting back, he jerked his hand away. The motion seemed to startle Kira, but he quickly captured her chin.

Telling himself he was only doing this so she'd think twice about provoking him, he slipped his other hand between her elbow and waist and lowered his mouth to hers.

Whatever emotions Kira had detected flickering in the black depths of Cole's eyes escaped her thoughts at his lightning-quick move. One minute he'd been lazily seducing her; the next thing she knew, her chin was captive to his large, callused palm, and her lips of his hot, hungry mouth. And damned if she didn't like them both.

Responding was not an issue, but a reality. Kira tried to temper the urge for enthusiasm that seemed to overwhelm her common sense by keeping her hands clenched into fists at her side. His tongue pushed into her mouth. Her palms itched like mad to dive into his thick black hair. He released her chin and pulled her tightly against him as he deepened the kiss. She used all the restraint she had in her body to keep from grinding her hips against his.

But as his sensual assault on her mouth continued, she knew the battle was going to be a short-lived one. At this point, she couldn't quite remember why she'd been fighting him in the first place. She felt like a slowly melting candle, with her tongue as the wick. Pleasure cascaded into her mouth as his tongue slid against hers. The heat his touch created seemed to pour down her throat and throughout her body until she finally had to grab at his shoulders for support.

The urge to moan rose in her throat. She gave in and let herself relax against him. But her groan of passion became a squeal of fright when the door at her back gave way. As if he'd expected the sudden motion, Cole had pulled her tightly against him, his hand bracing the doorframe to keep them from falling.

Before she could clearly assess what happened, his warm lips grazed her earlobe.

"One office door open. And don't worry, I consider myself paid in full."

Kira pulled out of his grasp, half-surprised when he let her go. Her other emotion felt something like disappointment, so she didn't study that too closely. She was too busy trying to come up with an appropriately scathing reply. But she made the mistake of looking at him first.

He was breathtaking. Literally. The impact of seeing Cole under the unforgiving fluorescent bulbs in her office left her breathless. The hard planes of his face were that much leaner, the blunt sensuality of his full lower lip that much more inviting. A thin scar ran across his forehead. In the darkness she'd thought it a natural crease.

His black eyes, fringed with thick lashes that flashed almost a deep blue in the glare of fluorescent lights, fairly glowed as he looked back at her. She wanted to touch him, but when she lifted her hand, he shifted away. It was a slight movement. Barely more than a flex of a few muscles. So slight she might have missed the tiny reaction had she not been studying him so closely.

His rejection of her touch instantly brought to mind what they had shared in the dimly lit hallway. She had been swept away by his caresses, but not completely. Given his comment just now, she had no doubt he'd set out intentionally to remind her what an unprincipled bastard he was. And she'd been crazy enough there for a moment to have taken the lesson to heart. But he'd made one rather crucial mistake in his otherwise flawless plan.

He'd let her touch him.

During that supposedly cool, calculated kiss, while he'd been skillfully jimmying open her door, literally behind her back, Cole had become involved enough in his seduction to let her touch him.

Or had that been part of the plan?

No. She didn't think so. His instincts to pull away were too ingrained. She lifted her gaze back to his. There must have been something of what she was feeling in her expression, because his smug smile faded until his lips were pressed together in a hard, unforgiving line. If she didn't know better, she'd say he was angry.

But she was beginning to learn how to read him. He wasn't angry. He was . . . unsettled. Still, there was only one way to be sure. Test the theory.

So she said out loud the first thing she'd thought at looking at him in the full light of her office. "You're breathtaking."

He shifted his weight almost imperceptibly onto the balls of his feet. Warm. She took a small step toward him. His eyes narrowed, intently focusing on hers, willing her to stop. Warmer. She smiled at him.

"Kira." He said her name in the manner of a wolf issuing a low growl to warn a foolhardy predator that it better seek its prey elsewhere.

Hot.

"Cole," she responded, her eyes never leaving his. She took another minuscule step toward him, suddenly wanting more than anything to touch him. To stroke him and soothe whatever pain it was he harbored so closely and trusted no one to help him heal.

Her gaze was drawn away from his eyes, which glittered now with a suppressed emotion she was helpless to name, by his hands, which were slowly clenching and unclenching.

Her gaze shifted quickly back to his.

Burning hot.

Seemingly with a will of their own, her hands began to lift toward him. She was focused so intently on his eyes, willing him to let her in, willing him to let her ease him in whatever way he was able to allow her to, that his sudden move took her by complete surprise.

Like lightning, his hands shot out and grabbed her shoulders. Before she could blink, he'd whirled her around and pulled her back against him, his arms wrapped tightly in front of her, her own trapped beneath his.

His heart pounded hard against her back; the heat radiating from his body was almost tangible. His breath was hot and alive on the sensitive skin of her neck. But most disconcerting was the raging need she felt pulsing against her lower back. She tried to take several steadying breaths and to keep from pressing her backside into him. She failed on both counts.

He uttered a harsh oath in her ear, than captured her earlobe between his teeth. He pressed down, biting her gently, and Kira moaned.

"Dear God in heaven, what did I ever do to deserve you?" he whispered into her ear.

Kira didn't know if she'd been cursed or praised. She couldn't consider it too closely, though, because he'd begun to trace her ear with his tongue. "Cole, I—"

"Hush." He nuzzled her hair aside and kissed the bare patch of skin where her neck became her shoulder. His lips grazed her ear once more. "I'm only going to tell you this once, so listen to me. Don't look at me like you want to heal me, sweet lips. Don't make the mistake of thinking you can put your hands on me and make the hurt go away. You can't." He sucked her earlobe for a long moment, taking much of the harshness out of his words. "Not even you," he whispered.

SEVEN

Kira began to tremble. The message was clear. So why wasn't her body listening? Because her inner voice had heard the cry from Cole as clearly as it had heard Rio's cry for P.J. The urge to touch Cole hadn't been diminished by his warnings; it had only increased.

She tried to relax inside the encompassing strength of his arms. As he waited for her response tension tightened his entire body into a hard, coiled mass behind her. She did the best she could. But it was another long moment before she dared to speak.

"Is it so hard, Cole?"

His lips were pressed against the side of her throat as he let out a pained laugh. "You have no idea." His grip relaxed just slightly, and his lips gentled on her skin. "Yes, Kira, it's that hard."

"You know you can trust me." The words were quietly spoken, barely more than a whisper. His lips stilled.

He squeezed her tightly for a long moment, but Kira didn't mind. In fact, she reveled in the small gift of an honest emotion that was neither anger nor lust.

"Trust has nothing to do with this, Kira." As if sensing her retort, he reached up with one hand and pressed a rough finger against her lips. "I want the pain. I need it." He took a deep breath and let his finger rub softly back and forth over her lower lip. "I'm not even sure I can let you give me your body." She stiffened, but Cole continued. "Don't offer me anything else, Kira. I'll only turn you down. Save your strength and compassion for P.J. He needs it a lot more than I do, and he'll sure as hell appreciate it more."

Kira let his words play around in her mind for a minute. Cole didn't resume his slow assault of her neck. He'd all but stated that the only personal relationship he was willing to have with her was a physical one, and he'd barely consented to that. He'd made it excruciatingly clear that she would be the giver and he the taker. If she could handle that, then he was ready, willing, and most certainly able. But the decision would be hers.

Dear Lord, she prayed silently, when the time comes, let me make the right one. Out loud she said,

"I think maybe it's time we went out and introduced you to the other dolphins."

Cole apparently took her quiet statement to mean that she'd chosen to restrict their relationship to business, at least for now. Without another word he released her and stepped away. He stood in the open doorway with one hand on the knob.

Kira grabbed her purse and flicked off the light. She paused briefly and looked at Cole, his lean face once again cast in half shadows, then scooted past him, making certain she didn't brush against him in even the most innocent way.

When she didn't hear him close the door behind her, she turned back. He was still lounging in the doorway, his lips curved in that crooked half smile of his. So, the test in the doorway had been intentional. She headed on down the hall. "Don't bother locking it," she tossed over her shoulder, "I don't think I can afford the locksmith."

She was rewarded with a low chuckle.

Smiling, she swung her purse as she pushed through the door and headed for the water.

The night air was heavy, hot, almost oppressive. Kira dropped her purse on the counter of the equipment shack and flipped on the two floodlights directed at the cove. The intense white beams transformed the area into a brilliant false daylight. Kira switched them back off. The moon was fairly bright, with no clouds to speak of. Lots of stars.

Much better.

Without turning to see if Cole had caught up with her, she strolled down the central pier toward the platform anchored at the opposite end. It was at water level and was the base of operations when they worked with both the dolphins and children. Leaning on the railing at the other end, she knew immediately when Cole stepped onto the wooden planks behind her, though as usual he was as soundless as a jungle cat. She simply felt him.

As she sensed him nearing her she pointed toward a pair of fins slicing through the water several yards away. "That's Cutter on the left and Old Joe on the right."

Cole stopped directly beside her, leaning his forearms on the railing. She didn't turn to look at him, but from the corner of her eye, he appeared to be looking at the approaching dolphins.

"How can you tell them apart?"

Kira repressed a shiver at the rough sound of his voice. Would there ever be a time when he didn't affect her so . . . viscerally? *Yes*, came the immediate answer. As soon as she got P.J. back. After that, she'd never be disturbed by that deep voice again. She kept her gaze steady on the water. "Old Joe has a nick on his dorsal fin. In the daylight he's also a darker shade of gray than Cutter."

"So how do you know that's Cutter with him and not Rio?"

Kira's shoulders slumped slightly at the mention of Rio. "Because Cutter always pals around with Old Joe when the females aren't in this part of the cove."

"And?"

She turned to him, surprised that he'd picked up on her distress. "And because Rio hasn't left the gate to the canal since yesterday morning."

"Is he in imminent danger?"

She turned her attention back to the dolphins. "Paul rowed a boat out to him twice and fed him. He didn't eat much."

A moment passed, then Cole placed a hand on her shoulder and squeezed very gently. Kira felt a sudden burning behind her eyes at the reassuring gesture. Coming from Cole, it was doubly sweet. She had a sudden fierce wish that he'd pull her into his arms and let her lean into his sturdy frame for comfort and support, but she didn't dare initiate the contact. And for some odd reason, that infuriated her.

Kira stepped behind Cole and turned to lower herself down the short ladder to the platform. She needed comfort, and she sought it with the dolphins. She whistled a light shrill cadence, then knelt and leaned out over the water. Seconds later two smiling bottlenose dolphins broke the surface a mere inch from her outstretched hand.

Cutter emitted a rapid set of clicks and whistles while Old Joe swam in closer, looking for a possible treat.

"Sorry, fellas, I'm empty-handed." Her voice dropped to a whisper as she added, "Just needed some company." Cutter nudged Old Joe aside for his share of attention. He pressed his melon against her hand, and she stroked the protruding forehead gently. "How's your buddy out there?" As if they understood, both dolphins responded with a series of clicks and squeaks. Kira smiled, enchanted as always by the mammals' openness and affection. But despite their ever-present smiles, their rapid clicks and whistles told her they knew something wasn't right. She wished she could reassure them. "Would you tell Rio for me that I'd appreciate it if he'd eat a bit?"

It took several moments before Kira realized that tears were streaming down her face. Before she could shift her weight in order to wipe them away, a firm hand under her elbow lifted her to a standing position.

"I'll get him back, Kira." Cole ran a fingertip across her cheek as fresh tears edged over her lower lashes. "Tell them they'll have their friend back very shortly."

Kira sensed that Cole wasn't simply placating her. He knew something she didn't know. Her hands curled into fists, and she thumped him once on his chest. "You found something out and you didn't tell me right away?" Where the fury came from she didn't know; possibly she'd reached her stress limit. She didn't care why, only that she felt an overwhelming need to pound on something, and Cole was a very convenient target. She clenched her fists even tighter, the hands-off rule forgotten.

He caught her fists an inch from his chest. "What's gotten into you? I'm here to help, remember?"

Kira didn't back down. "Are you telling me that you don't have any information? That instead of telling me straight off and relieving me from the endless minutes I've spent going out of my mind, you deliberately took your sweet time doing other things like kissing me and, and—" She broke off as she realized how ridiculous she sounded. Letting the tension go completely, she would have swayed against Cole had he not been gripping her shoulders. "I'm sorry," she said roughly. "It's just been a long couple of days, and then I thought you weren't coming, and when you finally do show up, I don't know what to expect one minute to the next. . . ." She turned her gaze away for a moment to collect herself. "Never mind."

Cole turned her face back to his with a finger under her chin. "This your way of saying you missed me, sweet lips?"

It couldn't exactly be called a smile, but the slight

curve to his lips made her insides flip-flop and her heart speed up. "No. Dammit." The last was said with a reluctant grin. Her smile slowly faded as they stared at one another in silence. Even the dolphins had stopped their nervous chattering. "You have a plan, don't you?" Her voice was barely above a whisper.

"Yeah."

"What? When? How?"

"Whoa, slow down." He turned her away from the edge of the platform and stepped over to the ladder. Without warning, he gripped her waist and lifted her to sit on the edge of the shoulder-high pier. With grace and strength that left her slightly openmouthed, he placed his palms on the scarred planks next to her and levered himself up, angling his body till he sat next to her.

"Neat trick," she said, unable to refrain from commenting.

He shot her his patented semismile. "First thing they teach in smuggler school." His voice was a bit lighter than usual.

His expression flattened as her smile broadened. "Do you want to hear the plan or not?" he asked gruffly.

Thoroughly intrigued by the idea that Cole could be teased, Kira tucked her smile and the thought away for the time being. "Yes, I do. Have you found a way in?"

"I think so." His voice was all business now, but he kept his eyes trained on the cove. "I made a few inquiries, and I think you had the right idea about going in at night. His weakest security is just past the cove that fronts the main house. It's also the most direct route to P.J."

"Strange. Are you sure?"

Cole cut his eyes toward her. "Yes."

He didn't say anything else. Kira waited for a few moments, thinking he'd explain. Stupid assumption. She wondered how long it had been since someone questioned his word. She glanced at him. Forbidding, very forbidding. "That scowl might work on other smugglers, but I need a bit more information. I'm not doubting you, Cole. But you have to admit it's a bit unusual to leave such an easy entry unguarded. Could it be a trap?"

"You've read too many spy novels. Juan Carlos is a very arrogant man." Kira snorted. Cole lifted an eyebrow but continued blandly. "Except for the beach of the cove, the rest of the key is mostly reef and coral-edged. But the front of the main house is well lit and mostly glass. A man with his reputation takes precautions, but he also believes that no one would be foolish enough to approach him head-on."

"But we are."

"No."

"But I thought you just said—"

"*We* aren't. I am."

Kira turned to face him. "Oh no, you don't. No way will I let you go out there alone."

The crooked smile returned. "Worried about me?"

"No," she shot back, lying and not caring. "Men like you always land on their feet. It's P.J. I'm worried about. You don't know the first thing about dolphins, much less how to retrieve one."

"Men like me? What am I, Kira?"

"A survivor."

Cole flinched, an almost imperceptible move, but he knew she'd seen it. One of these nights he was going to have to stop provoking her. His expression bleak, he looked over at her. "Yeah," he said softly, "I am that."

She leaned toward him, then pulled back slightly. Cole was stunned by how much he wanted her to reach out and run her hands over him. The need was so strong, he had to actually fight the urge to shift away, to stand up and walk as far from her as necessary until the wanting and the needing stopped.

"Cole, you can't do this alone. You need me."

He gripped the edge of the pier to keep from grabbing her and shaking her. He wanted to shout at her to stop looking at him. To stop looking into him. Didn't she know she was killing him by inches? Each softly spoken word, each aborted move to comfort was like tiny knives slicing deeply into his gut. Into the depths of his soul.

But she was right, dammit. At least in this, he needed her. He took small consolation in the thought that her need for him was greater.

"If you go, you stay on the boat."

"Impossible."

Cole swore and slapped the pier between them. He ground his teeth when she lifted her chin. "I won't let you get close to Martinez's house, so just forget it, Kira. If you need to be in the water to help get P.J. onto the boat, then fine. But no following me, Kira." She either played this his way, or he didn't go.

If she insisted in putting herself in danger, then she could do it alone. He wouldn't be there to watch. Never again would he be forced to watch.

"When do we do this?"

Cole watched her warily. She hadn't exactly agreed to his demands. But she would. "Wednesday night. Juan Carlos will be off the island for several hours. It's our best shot."

"That's only two days before the investors' program."

"I know. But it's the only way. Will P.J. be able to work that quickly?"

"I don't know. It depends on his attitude and how he's been treated. We have a specially designed boat that we use to do physical checks on some marine mammals in the wild. We can transport him back in the sling, and I can examine him without having to involve anyone else." Kira paused and looked down at her hands, twisting restlessly in her lap. "Right now I don't care if he's able to work with the kids for the investors' meeting. I just want him back safe and sound."

"If he's in the cove, and my information tells me he is, then we'll get him back."

Kira looked up. "Just where did you get this information?"

Cole's expression became shuttered, and she silently cursed. Didn't he realize that it no longer made a difference to her what he'd done, or who he'd been?

"I reestablished a few contacts."

Kira's eyes widened at the unexpected tidbit of information. She studied him for a moment. "There's something you're not telling me. If it concerns me or the institute, I have a right to know."

"You sure about that?"

A chill slithered down her spine at his ominous tone. But she had no choice. "Yes."

"Martinez did have inside help. I've tried every other scenario, Kira. It had to be one of your people."

Kira rubbed her hands on her arms to ward off the sudden shiver that raced over her skin.

"Who is it, Kira?"

Kira immediately pictured Paul. Smiling, laughing, incredibly loyal Paul. It just couldn't be. He'd have no reason to do it. "I don't know," she said quietly. She wondered if it sounded like a lie. It sure felt like one.

"Protecting the person puts everything you've worked for at direct risk, Kira. Juan Carlos might not appreciate being outsmarted. He might come back. Only this time . . ." Cole stopped when he realized Kira had turned a shade paler than death. "Aw hell." He slid over and pulled her into his arms. "Sorry," he mumbled against her hair. She balled up his T-shirt into her fists and pounded against his chest. This time he let her.

"I'm so scared." The words were spoken in the barest of whispers.

"I know." Cole wrapped one arm around her waist and pushed the other into her hair, cradling her against his chest as she cried. "Show me what to do, Kira. I'll get him back. Just show me how."

Kira didn't want to relinquish her spot in his arms. For the first time in many years someone was worrying about her and not the other way around. He'd taken her burden and put it squarely on his broad shoulders. She felt protected and cared for. It was intoxicating, addictive.

Her tears slowed, then stopped. Not ready to leave the sanctuary of his arms just yet, she maintained her grip on the front of his T-shirt. What she really wanted was to snake her arms around his waist and hold on to him for dear life, but she didn't dare. That he'd let her grab his shirt in the first place surprised her, and she knew she shouldn't push it. But she was feeling very vulnerable and very alone, and she freely admitted to herself that she wanted—no, needed—his strength and warmth.

She also realized just how much she wanted the right to reach out and touch him whenever she wanted, to hold him when the need arose, as he held her. Holding his shirt wasn't much, but it was a start.

She could feel his heart beating steadily under her fist. His body was hot under her bare legs, his shirt damp from her tears. Her senses were tuned to an almost painful pitch. She felt very much alive. And suddenly not so very alone.

"Kira?" His breath stirred the air near her forehead.

"What?"

"If you think you're up to it, I'm ready for my first lesson in Dolphin Rescue 101."

Kira smiled against his shirt. He was teasing her. Not badgering her, or provoking her, or trying to seduce her. Cole playful? She'd never have thought him capable of it.

She leaned back in his arms and looked up into his eyes. The corner of his mouth was actually curving into the closest approximation of a real smile she'd seen since that first night in the parking lot at Repo's.

"Okay, Sinclair. First thing you have to do is strip."

The curve deepened until an even row of white teeth flashed at her. "Sweet lips, I thought you'd never ask."

Kira almost fainted. One of these days she'd learn not to tease him. Lord, when he smiled like that, the man went from dark and dangerous to downright devilish.

Cole shifted her off his lap and stood, pulling her up beside him. They weren't touching, but she was so close to him, she could feel his heart beating.

"I don't suppose you're planning to get naked with me?"

Still trembling from the aftershocks of that sinful grin, Kira didn't dare voice the response that immediately sprang to her lips. She wouldn't provoke him further.

Would she?

She turned and headed for the equipment shack. Half a dozen steps later she swung around, continuing to walk backward down the pier, and said, "As a matter of fact, I am."

Her eyes widened in disbelief when Cole clutched the fabric stretched across his heart and fell backward into the cove, sending a geyser of water shooting into the air. Laughing, she started back toward the spot he'd just vacated but decided it might be wise to change into her suit while he was otherwise occupied. Besides, she thought, a wide grin on her face, if he wanted to meet the dolphins, literally dropping in on them was a surefire way to do it.

Kira closed the door to the equipment shack behind her, pausing a moment before twisting the lock. The night air was still muggy, and with the recent heat wave the water in the cove wouldn't be too chilly. Still, she was tempted to put on a diving vest. Not because she'd need it in order to swim with Cutter and Old Joe. Actually, the material most dive suits were constructed of made it difficult for the dolphins to use their sonar. They preferred bare skin or porous material. But the diving vest covered more of her than the ancient bathing suit she stored in the shed for emergencies.

Hoping the sun-bleached blue maillot still fit, she unbuttoned her shorts and let them drop to the floor.

"Am I in time to help?"

It was Kira's turn to grab her chest, only in her case, she wasn't playacting. She spun around to confront him, her ankles twisting in the shorts still puddled at her feet. Arms flailing, she grabbed the counter for support and barely managed to right herself before smacking chests with Cole. "Haven't you ever heard of knocking?"

He'd steadied her with one hand but let it drop

to his side when she spoke. "I thought you were impressed with my breaking-and-entering skills."

"Not when I'm on the opposite side of the door. You should have knocked."

"Should have. Don't you know by now that we smugglers don't play by the rules?"

Kira looked away from the grin curving at the corners of his lips. He was getting the hang of that smiling stuff way too quickly for her peace of mind. Biting back the urge to tell him to cut it out, she solved her problem by turning her back to him instead. "Do you mind?"

"What? Watching you undress? Never."

His smoky voice raised goose bumps on her skin. She shot a quick glance downward and blanched when she realized her tank top did little to cover her cotton bikini briefs. She'd certainly worn less on a public beach—but not in front of Cole. Her tightened nipples underscored the difference.

He made no move to leave, and she wished for the nerve to nonchalantly strip in front of him. It would serve him right. After all, he'd managed to do it in front of her. An image of his tightly muscled backside flashed across her mind. For some odd reason it just now occurred to her that his buttocks had been just as tan as the rest of him. A secret smile crossed her lips.

She wondered what he'd do if he saw that hers were too.

Emboldened by her train of thought, she kicked her shorts loose and bent to scoop them up. Letting them hang from her hands in front of her thighs, she turned and gave him a smile. Her mouth went dry, and whatever she'd been about to say became a distant memory. While she'd been daydreaming about his magnificent tush, Cole had managed to shuck his sodden T-shirt and jeans without a sound. "Is that another smuggler thing?" she asked, her voice breathy.

Cole glanced down at the black briefs clinging damply against his skin. "Is what a smuggler thing?"

Kira kept her eyes firmly on his as she spoke. Good Lord, was there a part of the man what wasn't magnificent? "The ability to do just about anything without making a sound?"

"It has come in handy once or twice." He shifted away from the counter and stepped toward her.

Kira clutched her shorts to her chest, suddenly unable to draw in a breath, much less move away from him. She studied the swirled pattern of black hair on his chest as if it contained some mysterious clue that her life depended on deciphering.

He leaned closer, crowding her against the counter. "Don't worry, Kira. When it counts, you'll always hear me coming."

She choked on the sudden gulp of air, then ran her tongue over her suddenly parched lips. A low noise escaped his lips. Half groan. Half growl.

"If you won't let me help you with your clothes, maybe I can solve the problem you're having keeping your lips wet."

Kira shivered, but not from a sudden chill. Then his mouth was on hers, hot and hard. Powerful tremors forced her to grip the counter for support. Cole lifted her by the hips and sat her in front of him, moving between her knees without waiting for permission. His lips never left hers. He slid his hands from her hips up her waist, bunching up her top as he went. His fingers were hot on her skin. He stopped just as his thumbs brushed the curve of her breasts.

Kira moaned, shifting restlessly but unable to break her grip on the Formica edge, as if she'd slip completely into unreality if she let go. Cole shifted his hands to her arms, not bothering to straighten her shirt as he slid them upward until his rough palms framed her head, his thumbs rubbing over her cheekbones. His eyes, black as coal but lava hot, held hers captive as he took the kiss deeper. When her lips parted on another moan, he invaded her mouth, raiding it, robbing her of any thought. He kept at it, seducing her mouth, her lips, her tongue, until she no longer cared that he was doing all the taking without letting her give in return.

It wasn't until he dropped his hands to her hips and hooked his fingers in her bikinis that she came back to some state of awareness. "Cole . . ."

He was busy devouring the side of her neck. "Mmmm?"

"We can't—"

"Sure we can," he interrupted, moving his lips along her shoulder, tugging her tank-top strap with his teeth.

"The dolphins," she said, then gasped when his teeth closed gently on the curve of her shoulder.

"What about them?"

She could tell he was answering automatically and would continue his carnal exploration until he'd covered every inch of her body—or uncovered it— unless she stopped him. It took a second longer to convince herself not to go on and let him. But she had to.

"I'm not going to make love to you on the counter of the equipment shack," she said, wishing she sounded a bit more forceful and a lot less breathless.

"Fine," he said, "just tell me where you want to go."

"I want to go to the dolphins."

He stopped then to look up at her, one brow quirked suggestively. "That's different, but I'm game."

"To work," she added, shifting restlessly under his erotic ministrations. Her control was rapidly eroding and she made one last effort. "Cole, stop. Please."

His hands and mouth left her skin simultaneously, the sudden loss of his touch almost causing her to tumble off the counter. He stepped away, but brought his face close to hers. "Okay, we'll go play with your fish. But I want you to answer a question first."

"What?" She maintained eye contact, but it was difficult. There was a storm raging in his eyes, but not of anger at her sudden change of heart. It was desire. Dark, hot, the intensity almost tangible. She almost wanted to apologize for stopping him. Almost.

"If we didn't have a rescue mission hanging over our heads, would you have stopped me?"

"That's hard to answer," she responded honestly, "since you wouldn't be here otherwise."

Cole stared at her for a moment longer. "I'll be waiting by the platform when you're ready."

He turned and walked away, leaving her to wonder how he would have answered the question if she'd added, "Would you?"

EIGHT

Cole pulled back on the throttle and eased the boat closer to the upcoming key. Once he was certain of their location, he turned his attention starboard.

Kira was perched on the side rail of the boat, balancing her weight easily even though the trip hadn't been completely smooth. The moon wasn't much more than a sliver, but it was a clear night and the sky resembled a swath of velvet scattered with diamonds. Cole grumbled silently that a little cloud cover would have been nice, but after an assessing glance at the waters ahead, his gaze soon returned to Kira. He'd barely been able to take his eyes off her since they'd left the canal at Dr. Dolphin's an hour earlier.

He watched the breeze whip tiny strands of hair around her face until one caught on her mouth. She snagged it with her finger, and he was forced to watch the silky piece slide across her lips. His hands tightened around the wheel as his body responded. Everything she did—sitting, breathing, staring—reminded him of the kiss they'd shared in the equipment shack two nights before. He shifted his attention away from her lips to the black cotton T-shirt she now wore. The moon cast the fabric a pale silver. Cole was riveted by the way it caught and clung to the fullness of her breasts. His fingers twitched as he remembered how soft they'd felt, how she'd responded even though he'd barely brushed his thumbs against them.

He shifted, trying to ease the growing discomfort between his legs. It didn't work. With a muttered oath, he tore his gaze away from her and put it where it belonged, on the snaking shoreline off the port side. He disciplined his mind to go over each and every detail of their plan. Nothing could go wrong. He simply wouldn't allow it.

Kira slipped off the railing and came to stand beside him. His body hardened further at her nearness. He clamped his teeth tightly together, disgusted with his increasing lack of self-control around her. What in the *hell* was he doing out here with her?

Suddenly he wished he'd never seen Kira Douglass or heard of her crazy scheme to rescue a damn five-hundred-pound fish. He could be at Repo's, emptying his soul into the sax right now instead of risking his life—not to mention his sanity—by getting himself involved in the exact type of activity that he'd sworn never to do again.

"How much farther to the rendezvous point?"

She kept her voice low; it barely reached his ears. He took one hand off the wheel before he'd even realized his intent. Instead of touching her, he aborted the instinctive move and rubbed his hand distractedly across his abdomen. "About twenty minutes."

"You're certain your friend will be there?"

"I wouldn't exactly call him a friend."

Kira sighed in barely concealed irritation. Cole fought his own smile, telling himself it was better to maintain distance between them. Though he wasn't sure if irritation was any better a barrier than frustration.

"Whatever you want to call him then." She angled a pointed look at him. "Though how you expect me to know anything about a person I just found out about *thirty minutes* ago is beyond me."

"I told you why I didn't mention him before."

"And I still don't like it."

"Well, that's just too damn bad," Cole shot back, allowing himself to be lured by the promised relief a good argument might bring to his nether regions. "You forget I saw your common sense in action in Repo's. I've got enough to deal with trying to rescue your damn fish without worrying about you."

He watched Kira's eyes sparkle with anger, her fists balled at her hips. He knew the fish remark would get to her. And damned if that didn't make him want to kiss her too.

"Your only obligation is to P.J. I can take care of myself."

Cole snorted, then made a smooth shift to the left, barely escaping the karate chop to the stomach she'd sent flying his way. He knew she was under a great deal of strain, but his role tonight was a bit trickier than she realized, and he couldn't afford to let her use him as a punching bag to ease her frustrations. Whether he deserved it or not.

Switching tactics, he tried to soothe her. "Kira, I know you think you can handle this, but Martinez is an unscrupulous bastard capable of doing just about anything to get what he wants." He paused, cursing under his breath when he saw her flinch. He should have known he'd screw this up. He was not a soother by nature. "Hell, Kira, you couldn't even take on Iggy. What makes you think you'd stand a chance against someone like Juan Carlos?"

Eyes blazing, with her hair whipping around her head like some wild Valkyrie, Kira turned on him, pushing her face up toward his. "That was different! The guy was shoving crickets in my face and trying to make me deep-throat his iguana's tongue!"

Cole cut the boat closer to shore and shut off the engine. As soon as he was certain they wouldn't drift into anything, he let go of the wheel and gripped Kira by the shoulders. Pushing his nose right up to hers, he whispered fiercely, "And Martinez makes Iggy look like Howdy Doody. After thirty minutes, you'd be begging to eat the damn iguana raw or anything else you had to do to get away from him." Her eyes widened at the violence in his tone. "You're not going with us." The fury in her eyes died down a bit, and Cole relaxed his grip. Softening his tone, he said, "You've taught me everything I need to know, Kira. Reese and I will get P.J. back to the boat. After that, it's your show."

He watched her swallow and groaned out loud when she moistened her lips before she spoke. "Reese?" Her voice was more croak than whisper.

Cole swore, but a corner of his mouth curved slightly. "You got it out of me after all. He won't be happy about that."

Her eyes narrowed. "I don't give a flying—"

"Shhh." Cole placed his fingers across her lips. "He doesn't have to know. If everything goes according to plan, you'll never meet him." He felt her biceps muscles contract under the hand he had on her arm. His other hand was still at her lips. He didn't move it away, even though he knew she wasn't going to speak. Rubbing his thumb over her bottom lip, he used every bit of his restraint to keep his mind on the topic at hand and off just how badly he needed to taste her again. The thought that this time he might not be able to stop at kissing was only marginal help. "We have it nailed down, Kira. Nothing will go wrong. I'd trust Reese with my life. Will you trust me with P.J.'s?"

She shifted her mouth away from his touch. "I thought you said he wasn't your friend."

"I did."

Apparently sensing he wasn't going to elaborate, she stepped away. He didn't let his hand drop. He wanted an answer. He just wondered if she knew how much he was laying on the line for her by taking responsibility for anything—anyone—besides himself. The seconds drew out to a minute, giving Cole too much time to think about just why he had agreed to this venture.

She turned her face to his. "I trust you."

His grip tightened for a moment as he steeled himself against the urge to pull her into his arms. Instead, he released her and twisted the key in the ignition. The motor sprang to life with a soft purr. He angled the boat slightly away from shore. "We'll be at the inlet in about fifteen minutes. When I give the signal, you take over the controls. From the moment we enter the inlet, hand signals only."

"Yes, Cole."

Cole shot her a dark look. "I'm trying to reassure you, so don't get smart-mouthed with me, okay?"

Kira raised her eyebrows, but her lips curved in a small smile. "Yessir."

Cole heaved a long-suffering sigh and ignored the throaty laugh that drifted back to him as she headed to the front of the boat. His sigh turned to a groan as he watched her prop her long, well-toned, very bare legs against the side rail.

"Cole?" she called softly.

"Mmm?"

"I've been meaning to ask you. Whatever happened to Elvis?"

The boat jerked slightly, and Kira had to grab the railing to keep her balance. "Cole?"

"I heard you."

A long pause. She'd expected a tossed-off answer, but a quick glance at him found him scrutinizing the shoreline of the key they were passing as if he expected an ambush, and she sensed she'd hit a sore spot. *Why?* Telling herself she was only pushing the issue because it would distract her from the mounting tension of the rescue mission, she swung off the seat and walked back to the console. "What happened to Iggy's pet?"

He kept his gaze pinned to the water. "How should I know?"

"You did hide him in Repo's that night to distract Iggy and the gang long enough to rig the bikes, right? Where did you stick him?"

"Why all the sudden concern? Who says he's missing?"

"Paul found a flier on his car the other night

with a picture of Iggy and Elvis asking for information on his return. He's even offering a reward, Cole."

"So? Maybe the damn thing ran away. Wouldn't you?"

She ignored the sarcastic comment. "Where did you hide him?" When he remained silent and turned his intense scrutiny back on the shore, Kira leaned across the console. "You didn't hurt the man's pet, did you?"

That got his attention. Cole swung around, his face an inch from hers. "It's a bit late to start worrying about him now, don't you think? Where was all this dripping concern when Iggy was shoving crickets in your face, huh?"

"You know I'm thankful to you for getting me out of there. But just because I didn't want to kiss the damn thing doesn't mean I wanted you to hurt it!"

Cole's eyes widened a fraction, then narrowed dangerously. He turned away, his clamped jaw and squared shoulders telling her he was obviously insulted. For a brief moment she could have sworn he'd even been hurt by her assumption. Cole the invincible?

A few minutes passed while she mulled over that startling idea. She even took a step back toward the front of the boat, but she just couldn't leave it alone. She waited until he had to check the water in her direction, then said softly, "Just tell me what you did with him." He looked at her, a muscle in his jaw twitching as if he was fighting the urge to answer. "Please? I won't ask another question about it, I promise."

Cole cut his gaze quickly to his left, checking the shoreline, then back at her. "You never learn, do you?"

"What do you mean?"

"Don't make promises when you don't know all the facts, Kira." He leaned closer, his eyes boring into hers with an intensity that was just this side of mesmerizing. "And don't ask questions unless you're really ready for the answers."

Kira bristled at his implication but kept her gaze locked on his. "So, tell me."

Cole straightened away, cutting the engine back and turning the boat toward what looked like a solid shoreline. "I gave him to Axe." Cole slanted a quick glance her way, a sardonic smile curving his lips at the question he must have seen in her eyes. "Okay, sweet lips, I'll give you one. Axe is Repo's cook."

Kira's mouth dropped open. Unable to prevent the question from slipping out, she blurted, "Repo serves food?"

Cole maneuvered the boat into an almost invisible slit carved into the mangroves that made up the shoreline. "Pay attention, you'll have to steer this thing back out of here." She would have responded, but as soon as the boat was fully into the tiny inlet, he motioned to her to keep quiet.

Feeling as smoothly maneuvered as the boat he'd just tucked neatly away, she shoved her fists into the pockets of her shorts and took her place next to him. The inlet wasn't much more than a tidal pond sunken into mangroves and dead coral. She spied a small pier, one end dipping perilously close to the water, proving it hadn't seen any recent use.

Cole steered the boat toward it. Once alongside, Kira threw a rope around the most stable-looking piling. Cole leaned forward and grabbed the end of the rope, motioning Kira to step back to the console. They switched places, and Cole grabbed the bags of equipment and gear they'd packed earlier. With the underwater transponder, oxygen tanks, and various other tools Cole felt the need to carry, it wasn't a light load. He lifted them onto the dock, away from the sunken end, with ease.

Turning back to Kira, he nodded, then placed his palms on the pier as if to lever himself up. But he paused for a moment. Kira held her breath, watching the play of muscles as they flexed under his black T-shirt. In that split second it hit her. She didn't want him to go. She didn't want him put at any risk by trying to get P.J. back. It struck her with the force of a Gulf hurricane that he had become more important to her than P.J., her institute, even herself.

When or just how it had happened, she didn't have the luxury of thinking about. The simple fact was she did care. And he had to go. But he didn't have to go alone.

As if he'd read her mind, he shot a look over his shoulder. In seconds he'd wrapped and knotted the rope around the piling and was at her side. Her hands were wrapped around the wheel and throttle, but his hands were on her face, holding her motionless a mere breath away from his own.

"I'll get him back," he whispered. "Do it like we planned, Kira."

Had he spoken? She felt the fierceness of his tone almost more than she actually heard the words. Her hand shot up to caress his face, to savor one touch before he left, but she broke off the movement with her palm a whisper away from his cheek. When she spoke, she was careful to keep her voice soft. "Don't do anything too risky."

Cole's eyes, flat and emotionless a moment ago, gleamed for a split instant. "There's always a risk, Kira."

His searing gaze held hers intently, commandingly. Suddenly Kira knew they weren't talking about Juan Carlos, or tonight's mission. But she couldn't shake the feeling of imminent danger in the hours ahead.

She reacted on instinct; her hand trembled violently next to his cheek but didn't touch him. "Come back, okay? P.J. or no P.J., you come back to me, Cole Sinclair."

If his gaze had been hot a second ago, it flashed in response to her heated whisper with an emotion so primitive, her entire body began to shiver uncontrollably.

As if with great force of will, he took hold of her hand, still next to his cheek. Never shifting his gaze from hers, he pressed it firmly against his mouth; his lips on her palm were a brand on her skin. Folding her fingers down into a fist, he stared at her a moment longer. Then, with a nod, he turned and leaped noiselessly onto the high side of the rotting pier.

Kira's heart was pounding wildly against her chest. Breath she couldn't spare remained locked inside her lungs, useless, as she watched the pier rock dangerously under his weight.

He quickly arranged the gear on his back, then untied the rope and tossed it down to her. He made the previously arranged hand motion telling her to head to the location he and Reese would attempt to steer P.J. to. Then he was gone.

Kira dropped anchor around the bend from the spot where Juan Carlos's hacienda-style home overlooked the natural cove in which P.J. was being held. She tugged hard at the rope, making certain it was tight, then moved to set up the transmitting device. She'd agreed with Cole that she had to keep the boat out of direct sight, since Martinez had powerful floodlights angled toward the water at the cove's entrance that could be switched on without warning.

She glanced starboard toward the shoreline, barely one hundred yards away. It was dense with stunted palms, sea oats, and mangroves. The old coral that lined the shore was jagged enough to prevent all but the very foolhardy from attempting to beach there. The information Cole had uncovered—probably from Reese, she now assumed—had shown this location to be the least patrolled, while still keeping her close enough for the sound of Rio's signature whistle to travel. Cole had reluctantly agreed that she should have a backup transponder in case he was able to free P.J., but for some reason they were separated. Kira shuddered at the thought of something happening to Cole. . . .

She yanked her mind from that destructive path. She set up the equipment, checked to make sure the signal was transmitting, then lowered the speaker quietly overboard, letting it sink a few feet before tying off the rope to keep it from drifting. Nothing was going to go wrong. Reese and Cole would enter the cove underwater, dive down to the underwater gate in the fence that closed in the cove, and release P.J. Reese would slink off to remain mysterious somewhere, and Cole would take the small inflatable raft Reese was providing to meet her at the boat. With P.J. hopefully following close behind.

She focused on seeing P.J. again, repeating over and over that it would be okay. She quickly moved to the rear of the boat to check on the tarpaulin sling stretched across the cutaway section of the boat. Providing P.J. was healthy, she'd signal him to leap onto the sling just as they'd done dozens of times before when they performed routine medical checks. Only this time, he'd stay in the sling, with her keeping him wet, until Cole had steered them safely back to the institute.

Nothing could go wrong.

A split second later gunshots shattered the silence of the almost moonless night with a deadly staccato matched only by the sudden acceleration of her heartbeat.

Kira ran to the console and grabbed the marine binoculars, then moved to the front of the boat, aiming the powerful lenses up the coastline toward the opening to the cove. Not that she could see anything in the dead of night, but her protective instincts toward Cole and P.J. propelled her to action—she couldn't just stand there, wringing her hands.

She strained to make out any movement on the water, wanting to see that inflated raft so badly, she was afraid she'd miss it for the tears misting her eyes. After a few moments of deafening silence, a burst of gunfire rang out again. Kira dropped the binoculars, her hand pressed between her teeth to keep from shouting Cole's name. Something had gone wrong.

Deadly wrong?

She quickly checked the transmitter. It was working. She checked the illuminated dial on her wrist. He was late. She went aft again and leaned out over the end of the boat, straining to see any movement coming in her direction. Nothing.

For a split second she thought she saw a dark shadow, but it didn't reappear, and she decided it was just a wave capping. She checked her watch again, debating the merits of sending out a low-whistled signal to P.J. that would make him leap out of the water. If he was free and heading her way, she'd be able to see him leap, but it might also make him a target if any of the gunmen were giving chase. Rational thoughts fought with chaotic emotions. She couldn't risk giving the signal. What had gone wrong? How long should she wait before taking some sort of action? Had Cole been hurt?

She blocked the riot of questions from her mind and checked her watch again. He was very late now. There had been no gunfire for several minutes. She didn't ponder all the ramifications of that, as she determined that it might be safer now for her to go after Cole.

She flipped open the trunk in the back of the boat and lifted out her diving gear. She picked up the oxygen tank she'd stowed away earlier, before Cole's arrival at Dr. Dolphin, then decided it wasn't that far to shore. It would only slow her down. If Cole was still out by the gate . . . Even with full diving gear she couldn't get to him. He had the light she'd need to guide herself that far in the dark.

She stowed the tank back in the trunk and quickly shed her shorts and shirt. She straightened the straps of her swimsuit and swore under her breath when they twisted further under her shaky ministrations. Despite Cole's inflexible rule that she was to stay on the boat no matter what, Kira had felt it important to be prepared for any possibility. In this case, she hated being right.

She tucked her sneakers inside the elastic leg bands of her suit, then slipped on the flippers, mask, and snorkel. Diving gloves were the last to go on. Taking one more look toward the cove and seeing nothing, she slid into the water. Shivering despite the warmer-than-average temperature, she headed for the shadowed shoreline.

Minutes later she slowed and began to tread water. Carefully, she reached down and removed one of her flippers. She tossed it onto a large piece of coral barely jutting above the water. The other flipper followed. Just as carefully she worked to put on her sneakers. It took a few minutes and many mumbled oaths, but once she had them on, she carefully approached the shore.

Her knees and elbows were bleeding, and there was a nasty scrape on her thigh, but she finally made it onto dry land. She tucked her snorkel and mask inside the gnarled roots of a dense mangrove patch and carefully picked her way toward the cove. The dense undergrowth wasn't any kinder to her bare skin than the coral had been, but she barely noticed the pain. She edged around another stunted palm tree that hung out over the water, then ducked back inland for a few yards. Once she was able to climb through the tangle of mangrove roots back to the edge, she scanned the shoreline. She blinked once, then twice. The raft was there, bobbing against the coral. And if she wasn't mistaken, it was occupied.

Oh, Lord, Cole!

The black shadow draped haphazardly across the small raft didn't move so much as it shifted with the movement of the water. Almost as if he were asleep. But as Kira made her way frantically toward it she had no doubt that Cole was unconscious. Had he been shot?

She stumbled twice, biting the inside of her mouth to keep from crying out, and finally made it to the raft. Mindful of its precarious position, she grabbed at the rope, securing it to a small tree, and guided herself until she could lean against the rounded side. The raft was black and made of a heavy rubberized canvas.

"Cole?" He was on his stomach, his face turned

away from her. She quickly checked for water in the boat. There was none. He hadn't drowned. She pulled off her diving gloves and reached a trembling hand toward his neck.

Placing her fingers against the side of his neck, she felt a pulse. A strong pulse. She shifted her weight carefully until she was almost completely inside the two-man boat. She carefully ran her hands over his back and down his arms, checking for . . . she didn't know. Bullet wounds? Kira shuddered, figuring it was the danger of the situation that made her feel strangely detached from Cole, even with her hands on his body. She scrutinized the sodden black T-shirt, but the color made it impossible to discern if he was bleeding.

Not stopping to consider what she'd do if he had been shot, she leaned over him and ran her hands down his legs, encased in black neoprene diver's trunks that ended above the knee. She felt a strap of some kind around his calf. Figuring it might be a knife that she could use to cut away his shirt or pants if necessary, she stretched as far as she could to try and unbuckle it. She'd just gotten it loose when Cole surged to life under her. If she hadn't grabbed his arm, she'd have fallen back into the coral-laden water.

"It's okay, it's just—" She broke off when she swiped the hair out of her eyes and realized the ones staring back at her were blue. Or maybe gray. It was hard to tell in the dark. But one thing they definitely weren't was black.

"Who are you?" she blurted out.

"I might ask you the same question, luv." His accent sounded strange, not quite British, but he didn't give her the time to figure it out. "Hand me the knife like a good bird, then we'll get around to introductions."

Still stunned by the magnitude of her mistake, Kira held out the sheathed knife without even a word of protest. Then it struck her. "Reese," she whispered.

NINE

Kira noted the infinitesimal moment of surprise before Reese's face became an unreadable mask. "You *are* Reese." She grabbed his arm and yanked it. "Where's Cole? What happened to him? Tell me!"

The big man—blond she now realized as she looked at his eyebrows, though his wet hair looked much darker—carefully removed her hand from his arm. "Your concern is touching, but if you want to know how Cole is, then I suggest you get back to the damn boat you weren't supposed to leave in the first place and ask him yourself."

He'd started out in a soft tone, but by the end he was whispering so fiercely, she leaned away from him. It occurred to her that maybe there was a good reason Reese hadn't wanted anyone to know who he was. But he wouldn't hurt her. Not if he was a friend of . . .

Cole's description of their less than amicable relationship played back in her mind. She glanced at the water behind her, then back to Reese. He was staring at her, no trace of emotion visible in his light eyes. Still in a state of semishock from the tangled events of the evening, she found herself unable to concentrate on what he'd just said. Instead, she said the first thing that struck her. "Are all smugglers as good as you two at hiding their thoughts?"

His jaw twitched lightly. "Is that what Sinclair told you?"

"He didn't tell me anything about you. I sort of found out your name by . . . accident."

"I don't believe this," he muttered, rubbing his shoulder. With a pained sign, he said, "To answer your earlier question—we tripped an alarm and all hell broke loose. I assume Sinclair made it back to your boat. That is, if you didn't run off when you heard gunfire."

Kira's eyes narrowed. She didn't much like this man. Whoever or whatever he was. "No. I waited, but he didn't show up. So I left the boat anchored and swam to shore to see if he needed my help." She ignored Reese's disbelieving snort. It had finally sunk in that Cole was probably back at the boat with P.J.

by now, and she was wasting time talking to a surly Australian. "Are the bad guys gone?"

He arched a blond brow. "So now I'm a good guy?"

"What I meant was, if we aren't in any danger, I'd appreciate it if we could heave ho and get back to the boat. I have a dolphin to take care of."

His eyes narrowed, cynicism replaced by disgust. "Yeah, he almost gets blown sky-high, and you're worried about a fish. Figures." He shook his head. "I've been trying to lure him back for over a year. Couldn't figure out how a simple Sheila pulled it off." He focused those eerie light eyes on her again. "But you're a cocky one. Guess you just nagged him to death." He snorted. "American women."

Kira couldn't decide which insult to address first, but she hadn't missed the reference to the danger they'd been in that night. She had to get back to Cole. "Go to hell."

"Already been there," he shot back.

"Fine then, go back to Australia. At least there you won't have to worry about being threatened by some American 'Sheila.' " She turned to leave, but was immobilized by a firm grip on her arm. Kira wondered why Cole's touch had affected her so intimately, while with Reese she simply had a burning desire to kick him between the legs.

"I'll take you back to the boat. Keep quiet."

"Yes, sir," she said mutinously, once he'd let go

of her. She could have sworn he snarled, but she decided to let it go and just get back to the boat and Cole.

She saw him start to reach for the small motor with his right arm, check the movement, then use his left instead. She'd been so angry at him, she'd forgotten she'd found him unconscious. "You're hurt, aren't you?"

"We'll be there faster if you sit still," was all he said.

There was a long stretch of silence while he maneuvered the boat off the coral. They had gone several hundred yards away from the cove when he spoke again. "Can you steer this thing?"

"Yes. Why, is your injury serious? Let me help." She started to shift off her side of the raft, but Reese raised his hand, signaling her to stop.

"Follow the shore about another hundred yards, then head straight out. The boat should be in front of you."

"Okay. But you'll have to move over—"

"I was wrong to get Cole involved tonight," he said abruptly. "Don't let him follow me. Just tell him, mission accomplished."

"Involved in what? What mission? I thought—" She never finished the sentence, because Reese had disappeared over the side. Alarmed, she looked out over the water in the direction he'd dived, but he didn't surface. Just as she was about to head closer to shore, she saw his head break the surface near the coral. He waved her off. She turned the tiny raft around and headed in the direction of the boat. She prayed Cole was there with P.J. and that both were okay.

One thing was for certain. P.J. was going to be much happier to see her than Cole.

She spied the boat and wanted to whoop out loud when she was close enough to make out a dorsal fin protruding from the tip of the sling. P.J.! She settled for pumping her fist in the air and opened up the tiny-horsepower engine to its max, not caring if she made a bit too much noise. In the next instant a large black shadow loomed over the side of the boat.

She could see him gripping the railing and couldn't stop the stupid grin from plastering itself all over her face even when he said, his voice filled with more than a little menace, "Don't you ever follow instructions?"

She threw him a line, which he grabbed in the air, dragging her the last few feet. He reached down and pulled her into the boat. His strength still amazed her, and his touch had a wildfire effect on her pulse.

"Where in the hell have you been?"

"I can see you're okay," she said dryly. "How's P.J.?"

"I checked the signs you told me to look for. He

seems to be fine. Hard to tell with that damn smile always pasted on his face. I just wet him down, but we need to get a move on."

As anxious as she was to reunite with P.J. and make sure he was all right, Kira was surprised at her sudden reluctance to turn away from Cole. Apparently, she did wear her emotions on her sleeve, because his fierce expression gentled a bit. He reached up to run a finger along the side of her face, pushing back the ragged snarled strands.

"You okay?"

His voice was a deep baritone that vibrated through her skin straight to her heart. "Well, I lost a few points to the coral, but I'm all right. Why, worried about me?" She bit back the urge to grin, even though she felt like shouting. Somewhere under that tough hide, he cared for her. And that was the difference. Cole was a man who'd locked away his soul because something had harmed it so badly, he couldn't risk exposing it again. Whereas Reese apparently had no soul at all. That reminded her of the message she'd promised to deliver. "Reese said to tell you mission accomplished."

Cole's eyes fairly glittered in response to that bit of news. "You have the raft," he said, as if just remembering how she'd arrived. "I'm playing nursemaid to a fish, and you're out gallivanting around with Reese?"

Given Reese's comments, she figured something

else was going on tonight besides a dolphin rescue. She'd question him on that later, but right now she needed to know something else. "Jealous too?"

Cole yanked her up against his chest. "You just don't know when to quit, do you?"

This time she couldn't hide her smile. For all his fierceness, he was holding her against him, cradling her, as if determined to keep her near him. Safe. "Apparently not," she said softly. "So why don't you stop yelling and shut me up?"

Cole looked down into eyes that were sparkling with challenge and . . . desire. His mouth was on hers before he gave it conscious thought. She moaned, and he tried to tell himself it was that soft noise that put him over the edge without a fight. But his tongue was deep inside her mouth by then and he stopped caring why or how he got there.

He pulled her closer, leaning back against the console and tugging her between his legs. She was sweet and wild and so damn hot he couldn't have taken his mouth from hers if his life depended on it. He moved his hands down her back and pulled her hips even closer. He began to rock her gently against him as he managed to leave her lips for the soft curve of her neck. He felt a pressure against his chest and realized it was her hands, trapped between them, curling into fists.

He couldn't stop the rumbling moan in his throat. Kira gasped, and his lips were on hers, catching her breath. He felt his control slowly dwindle with each murmur she made. It was a shock to him just how badly he'd come to want her. He needed to feel her not-so-soft hands on his skin. In his hair. Raking down his back. Grabbing his hips. He needed her to touch him in a way he'd never needed to be touched. In a way he'd always needed to be touched. In that moment he wanted to give himself to her, trust her, body and soul.

P.J. chose that second to start a running string of clicks and whistles that even to Cole's untrained, preoccupied ears sounded unnatural.

Kira tore herself from his arms but didn't run to P.J. immediately. Both of them were breathing heavily, staring at each other. If his expression mirrored hers, which he was afraid it did, they both looked a bit awestruck. Her soft gaze slowly focused as she continued to stare at him. She wore her emotions so plainly, it was almost painful to him to observe the transformation. Insecurity, pain, fear, all rushed in to fill the momentary breach in his control. He wished she hadn't sensed the barrier he'd crossed.

But she had.

P.J. began to squirm, and she finally looked away, going quickly to the restless dolphin. Cole ruthlessly shoved the whole matter from his mind as he turned back to the console. In quiet, efficient movements he went about securing the gear and pulling up the anchor. A few minutes later he started the engine and called over his shoulder, "All set back there?"

"He's a bit shaken up, but he'll travel all right, I think."

A bit shaken up. If she were describing him, it would've been a gross understatement. Cole watched for a moment as she switched on a small battery-powered lamp and aimed it at the dolphin's shiny gray body. She doused P.J. with water from a large sponge, crooning softly to him. Damn, but that soft voice sounded good floating through the night air.

Cole had forced his attention back to the engine when her voice stopped him cold.

"Will Reese be all right?"

Cole stiffened. "Why shouldn't he be? He said the mission was accomplished, didn't he?" Cole knew he sounded unnecessarily harsh. He was getting real tired of hearing Reese's name on her lips.

"I think he was hurt back there. I found him passed out in the raft. I . . . I thought he was you."

That last part had faded to a choked whisper, and Cole turned back to face her. He didn't speak right away. The idea that she'd been worried enough to go after him, to rescue him, created a warmth deep inside him. Instead of lecturing her on the reasons she should have stayed put in the first place, he asked, "Why didn't you bring him back to the boat?"

"I thought I was doing just that. He wasn't very cooperative."

Cole thought he detected a slight sarcasm there, but didn't call her on it.

"Apparently you guys take it as a real affront to be rescued by a woman. My knowing his name didn't go over too well, either."

Cole grinned at the image of Reese having to deal with Kira. "I can imagine it didn't. Where is he?"

"He came back about halfway, gave me directions, the message for you, then dove overboard. The last I saw him, he was headed back toward Martinez's." She didn't mention Reese's request that Cole not follow, certain it would only prove counterproductive.

Cole swore softly and looked back in the general direction of the hacienda. He turned and found Kira staring at him with a strange, almost apprehensive look on her face. He wasn't close enough to see the expression in her eyes, but he'd bet the bank they were full of questions. Questions that their kiss might make her think she deserved the answers to.

In the end it was the realization that he couldn't give her what she wanted—deserved—that decided him on his course of action. "Reese is a big boy," he said tersely. "He knows what he's doing." Yet Cole made a lingering study of the shoreline before turning the boat out toward the open water.

It was almost four in the morning when Cole turned the boat in to the canal leading to Dr. Dolphin's cove. He rubbed the back of his neck, resisting the urge to look back at Kira. He could feel her watching him. Again. He didn't turn to look at her. He wished he didn't want to.

He told himself to be thankful she'd remained quiet on the trip back, using the time to examine P.J. instead of peppering him with questions about his past. He could still taste her. He wanted to taste her again.

Kissing her like that had been a damn stupid thing to do.

In less than an hour his responsibility to her would be over. To hell with getting paid. He'd known from the start that he wasn't in this for the money. He told himself he owed that quarter-ton fish a big one for his timely intervention. He flicked a glance at his watch as they passed through the electronically operated gate in the cove's fence. Thirty minutes, one hour tops, and he'd be on Highway 1 heading for his houseboat. Or maybe Repo's. He hadn't had much of a chance to play any music lately. Relief was in sight. So why did he feel like breaking something?

He'd have to worry about that later. As they cleared the gate P.J. started squirming and setting up a ruckus.

"Cole, stop the boat."

He did as Kira asked, then swung around to see if she needed any help with the excited dolphin.

"I was going to put him in isolation for a while,

but I think he's fit enough for a reunion. And I doubt we have a choice at this point. Turn the boat so it faces the dock."

Once he'd done it, Kira lowered the sling closer to water level. She lifted the bucket of water she'd been dipping the sponge in and dumped it over P.J., careful to avoid his blowhole, making him as slippery as possible. She then gave him the hand signal to back out of the sling, but P.J. was a step ahead of her. In seconds he was surging across the cove.

P.J.'d been in the water only moments before Cole and Kira were drenched by a pair of dolphins arcing in a series of high leaps. The whistles and clicks were almost deafening.

Cole looked at Kira to see her laughing and pumping her fists in the air. He grinned. She turned to him, her face lit up in a way that made his heart ache.

"Thank you, Cole," she said, her eyes shining with joy and unshed tears.

No, he didn't want her money. As far as he was concerned, her account with him was now paid in full.

The dolphins were speeding back and forth in a frenzy of motion around the cove, leaping in perfect unison over and over until the boat had over an inch of water in the bottom.

"We'd better get the boat in," he called to Kira. She didn't answer right away, her attention totally

Donna Kauffman
178

on the dolphins. He allowed himself the luxury of
absorbing the glow that fairly emanated from her.
She might be stubborn, and rush into things without
a care to her safety. But she was also warm, caring,
honest. And, ultimately, giving.

He should know. He'd been doing a lot of taking.

He wanted to stand near her all night, any night.
But the time had come for him to leave. Judging
by how his gut knotted at the thought, it was past
time.

He kept the boat at the slowest trolling speed he
could and steered them to the dock they'd left hours
earlier. It seemed a lifetime ago. He looked back to
find her attention had shifted from the dolphins to
him. She wasn't smiling anymore.

He suddenly wished they had met a lifetime ago.
Before he'd given his life to the gunrunners and
drug peddlers, before Cuba, before Felicia. Before
the explosion and flames and shredded bodies had
rained down on him, before the yawning hellhole of
helplessness had swallowed him whole . . .

He spun away from her and went about gathering
his gear. He lifted it to the dock, then leaped up
after. Kira was on the dock behind him before he
could lend her a hand. Probably just as well they
didn't touch again anyway.

He made it to the equipment shack, then thought
better of going inside. He stowed the gear that

belonged to the institute on the outside counter. He knew she was right behind him. He also knew that simply walking away was out of the question. No matter how appealing that cowardly solution seemed at the moment.

He was no hero, but he was no coward, either. Besides, there was one bit of business left to discuss. With a tight hold on his rioting emotions, he carefully blanked his expression, hoping like hell he'd been successful, and turned to face her.

She was leaning against the door, arms crossed, as if she'd known he'd turn back to her all along. Instead of making him angry, it made him want to smile. He did neither.

"I don't imagine you'll have to worry about any revenge attempt from Martinez," he said, his voice rough. "The dolphins should be safe."

"How can you be so certain?"

"Let's just say there was another agenda besides ours at work tonight, and I imagine a lost dolphin is the last thing on Juan Carlos's mind right now."

Kira nodded, her expression distracted, as if the dolphin's immediate welfare wasn't uppermost on her mind. Before Cole could speak, she lifted her gaze to his and said, "I know I thanked you back on the boat. But I want to say it again. Thank you for bringing him back, Cole." Even in the shadows her eyes shone bright with tears. She looked down and scuffed the toe of her ruined sneaker in the gravel.

"We, uh . . . we never exactly got around to deciding what I owe—"

"Don't, Kira." His voice was no more than a bare rasp.

She looked at him then. "I have to. You're leaving." Her voice caught on that last word, but she refused to look down.

Cole swore under his breath. Damn her for trying to make this easy on him. He wanted yelling and bitching.

"Yeah, I am." He let his gaze roam over her, noticing for the first time the streaks of mud and grit that clung to her bare legs. Cole started toward her, thinking only that she was probably more banged up than she'd let on and wanting to get a closer look. She took a step away from him.

The fact that it had been instinctive rather than intentional stopped him cold. "You're hurt, aren't you?" He felt the anger rise in him, blessedly erasing the tension and frustration of moments ago. This emotion was much easier to handle. Heedless of his earlier decision not to touch her, he stepped closer, almost crowding her against the door. He lifted her arm and looked at her elbows, then crouched down to look at her knees. It was then that he noticed that what he'd thought was dried muck on her thigh was in fact dried blood. Fear for her congealed into fury at her obstinacy. "Dammit, why didn't you tell me about this?"

"Stop shouting at me." She yanked her arm from his grip.

It was her quiet tone that took the wind out of his sails. "Those are coral burns, Kira," he said steadily, proud of the restraint he was showing. "You need to get them cleaned out."

"I know that." The words were spoken evenly, with no emotion. "It's not the first time I've tangled with a coral reef and lost, and it won't be the last." She looked him in the eye, her expression now one of near defiance. "I'll take care of them as soon as you're gone."

"The hell you will!" he wanted to shout. But he couldn't. Her tone made it clear that he had no right to order her around, much less care for her. And she was right. He'd given up any hope to that claim when he'd announced his intention to leave.

Emotions he wasn't prepared to deal with roiled violently inside him until he wanted to beg for mercy. And she just kept staring at him.

He clamped his jaw, near to gnashing his teeth as the hopelessness of the situation pervaded him. He needed her. Badly. More than anything he'd ever needed in his life. But he had nothing to give. Not to anyone.

And most especially not to her. She deserved a man with no holes in his heart, no decay in his soul.

"Cole, please—"

The rattle of the front gate stopped Kira's words. Cole spun around, instinctively shielding her from any threat. The sky was still more black than gray, so it took a moment for the intruder's shadow to separate from the general darkness.

"Paul?" Kira tried to push past Cole, but she might as well have moved a mountain. On tiptoe she peered over his shoulder. Paul stood, stock-still as if in shock, less than a dozen yards away. A split second passed, then he stumbled back a step, then another, before finally turning and running toward the gate.

"Don't, Taylor," Cole ordered. "It's over."

Paul skidded to a stop but took a long moment before turning around. When he did, Kira sucked in a breath at the look of guilt and grief carved in his young, handsome face.

"Don't you think she at least deserves an explanation?"

Paul kept his gaze on Kira. "Yeah," he said softly. After a long, tense pause he said, "I'm sorry, Kira." His voice was choked with emotion. "I didn't know what else to do. I swear I didn't mean you or P.J. any harm. You've got to know that."

Kira did know that. Had suspected it all along. Which was why she was more disappointed than surprised. "For once, I really wanted to be wrong." She didn't realize she'd spoken aloud, until Cole reached back to pull her next to him, his expression changing from disgust to concern when he looked at her. "Why, Paul?" she asked, when she managed to drag her gaze from Cole's.

"You two have a lot to discuss." Cole moved away from her. Kira stiffened and turned to him. He'd already scooped up his gear and was walking toward Paul. But she fought hard against the urge to call him back. It would sound too much like begging. And she'd be damned if she'd do that.

He was a step past Paul when he stopped. In a voice just loud enough for her to hear, he said to Paul, "If she doesn't shoot you when you're done telling your story, see to it that she cleans out those abrasions."

Paul simply nodded.

Her eyes burned as anger swelled to mix with the shock and the hurt. She almost yelled at him that if this was his idea of a good-bye, then he could keep it. But the night had already thrown her one too many curves, and fatigue swiftly took priority over anger or anything else.

Ignoring Paul completely, she watched Cole stride out of the compound and out of her life as if he shattered hearts every day of the week. And damn her if she didn't feel sorry for him.

You don't know what you just threw away, Cole Sinclair, she said silently. You big, bullheaded idiot.

She heard him start his motorcycle and waited until she couldn't hear it anymore. When she was certain she could keep the tears from falling, she looked back at Paul.

"This had better be good," she muttered as she walked past him. When he didn't immediately follow, she motioned with her arm. "Well, don't just stand there. Let's go inside. My leg hurts like hell. You can spill your guts and clean out mine at the same time."

TEN

Kira turned past the sign to Sandy's pier, not bothering with her blinker. No one would be out this late at night. Or early in the morning, depending on how you looked at it.

A week had passed since Cole had strolled out of her life. And considering the punishing schedule she'd had, what with getting everything ready in time to pull off the investors' meeting and Paul gone, she'd barely been able to distinguish night from day. After a while she hadn't much cared. When she had managed to grab a few hours of sleep, she'd dreamed of Cole and awakened restless and edgy.

She stifled a yawn. The week would have been much smoother with Paul there to help. But that couldn't be. Sighing resignedly, she thought of Paul and how he'd helped Martinez in order to rescue his rebellious younger brother, Mickey, from the life that Juan Carlos had set him up in as a drug dealer. Paul had been so desperate that he'd swapped P.J. for Mickey. Kira understood, but she couldn't forgive Paul.

The rescue of P.J. had also led to the arrest of Juan Carlos, now being held without bail for an amazing list of crimes. Kira had made several attempts but could get no information on his son. At least Mickey was now having second thoughts about his lifestyle. Paul planned to take Mickey back to their parents' home in Tallahassee. She honestly wished them well. She dreaded having to find a new assistant, but she'd deal with that later.

Right now, her main concern was how to get on and off Cole's boat without him knowing she'd been there.

She shut off her headlights and killed the engine, drifting around the last turn. She let the car coast off the road onto the soft grass and quietly got out.

His motorcycle was parked in the lot at the end of the pier. That meant he was on the boat. Damn! She'd been hoping he'd be playing at Repo's or something.

She felt in her pocket for the envelope. The investors had come through with enthusiasm and open checkbooks. Dr. Dolphin was in the black for at least another year. And she knew that wouldn't have happened without P.J. or Cole. He not only deserved this, she reminded herself, he'd risked his life for it. She only wished it were more.

She walked as softly as she could, trying not to break the eerie stillness of the remote pier. The muggy night air didn't prevent the shiver from skating over her skin. It only heightened her sense of apprehension. Even the bugs were silent.

She was so intent on watching his boat for signs of movement, she tripped on the first plank of the pier. She froze in an awkward crouch, half expecting Cole to leap onto the dock and demand to know why she was here—and not entirely sure she wouldn't welcome his solid presence. It was too still. Her calf began to cramp. Nothing.

Perversely, that irritated her, and she felt like stomping down the pier to make sure he heard her coming. She'd lain awake nights and drifted off numerous times during the day when she had a million other things she should be doing, working up her nerve for this. Only now she had to admit her fear hadn't been the idea of confronting him. It had been the probability that she might not.

She gripped the railing, one leg lifted to climb on board, when she heard it. She froze.

It sounded like muffled yelling or arguing. It was coming from inside the boat. She leaped immediately onto the deck, going directly to the sliding doors. They weren't locked and slid open easily. Once inside, she had to pause a moment to focus.

The moon provided the only light, and she barely avoided colliding with the couch.

The noise had stopped when she'd entered the living room, but she'd been almost certain it had come from the back. Cole's bedroom. Heart pounding, she stood very still. Waiting. Her hands balled into fists, reminding her of the now crumpled envelope and her real reason for being here.

A horrible thought hit her. What if the sounds she heard had been Cole and another woman?

Dear Lord, she'd never thought of that. She felt incredibly stupid and not a little angry. Both at herself for thinking she could come here and not want to start things up again, and at Cole for letting another woman touch him. A woman who couldn't possibly love him the way she did.

There. She'd done it. She'd finally admitted it to herself. She loved Cole. Scarred heart and all. Damn him. Damn her.

She threw the envelope onto the bar and stormed toward the door, not really caring if they heard her or not. In fact, she wasn't too certain she wouldn't relish the confrontation. She yanked the sliding door closed.

"No! Oh, Lord, no."

The last word was drawn out into a tortured moan that made Kira's skin crawl even as she rushed back inside. All thoughts of who he might be with fled. *Cole!* She heard something crash behind the door across the room. She stumbled across a barstool and whacked her elbow on the doorframe in her haste to get to him.

She finally yanked open the door. Cole lay on the bed, twisting violently, the sheets, some white, some dark, tangled around his torso and legs. The moon came directly through his window, casting him and his surroundings in surrealistic shades of gray and white. A lamp lay broken on the floor. She hurried to the foot of the bed.

"Felicia!"

That stopped her, but only for a second. It was clear from his twisted expression and frantic thrashing that he was reliving something horrifying. His jaw was clenched, his face a mask of agony. She knew she'd be no match for him in this state, but she had to try. She couldn't let him do this to himself.

He moaned again. It was an inhuman sound. Dear Lord, what was he seeing? She leaned over the bed, as close as she could without getting clobbered by one of his arms, which he flung out in irregular intervals.

"Cole!" She shouted as loud as she could, hoping to get through to him. "It's Kira. Wake up!"

He kept writhing. He flipped over, the sheets binding even tighter around him. She grabbed at one and tried to untangle him from it. The white cotton mattress sheet had pulled loose and twined around his ankles. She yanked at the elastic edges until she managed to free one corner, then another. "Cole, it's me, Kira. Wake up." She calmly repeated the words over and over as she continued to try to free him, hoping the soothing sound would somehow help to quiet him and make it easier to shake whatever demons were controlling him.

She grabbed at the darker sheet twisted around his thighs and middle. She paused in surprise when she realized it was made of satin. Cole groaned again and flipped over just as she yanked. He landed on his back, no longer bound.

The satin sheet dropped to the floor. He was naked. Completely, gloriously, naked.

He groaned again, and she felt hot shame burn her cheeks. He was still in the grip of his nightmare, and she was standing there gawking. But she didn't know what else to do. Dump cold water on him? Just then he stilled, and she reacted instinctively. Taking advantage of his somewhat vulnerable position, she climbed on top of him, pressing heavily on his shoulders in an effort to keep him still long enough to wake him up.

Even in her anxiety to wake him, she couldn't ignore the feel of him. Or the impact the contact made on her. His skin was hot and damp against her palms, his deltoid muscles bunching tightly under her grip. She knew she had only seconds to get through to him before she risked being tossed across the room. She leaned close to his head, which was turning restlessly back and forth. Finally she pushed her face into the sheet next to his neck, using her head as a block to keep him still. She turned her lips next to his ear. "Cole, it's Kira. Wake up. Please."

She found herself instantly sitting upright, astride his hips, looking down into eyes so dark, they were almost demonic. His grip on her arms was painfully tight, and even now, he was preventing her from touching him.

"Cole! It's me, Kira. You're having a nightmare. You've got to wake up!" She could hear the desperation in her voice. He continued to stare at her. But he didn't move. Or let go. She licked her lips nervously, tasting the salt from the sweat on his neck where her lips had pressed. Was he awake? Did he know who she was? "Cole?"

It was the plaintive note in her soft voice that penetrated the violent red fog surrounding him. Cole grabbed for it like a life raft in a sea suddenly churning out of control. Even as he held on he couldn't shake the horrific vision that continued in front of his eyes, as if it took some sort of savage pleasure in making him a helpless witness over and over again.

"It's Kira," he heard her say again. But her voice wasn't the same now. Not soothing like before. Something had scared her. He had to get to her! Save her. No. No, it was Felicia he had to save. But she'd been blown up. Along with the children she'd been trying to save. They were all dead. He knew it, because he'd seen it. Again. And again.

The scene in front of him began to shift and blend until he became so confused he felt as if his skull would split open from trying to sort it out. He only knew he should have saved them. But there was nothing he could do. It was too late. He screamed out in frustrated anguish.

"Cole! Wake up!"

Images flew apart and slammed back together, but this time he controlled them. The horror vanished as he focused on the silvery eyes in front of him.

Kira.

Confusion crept back in. She was here. With him. In a bed. His bed. Her clothes were on. His were not. What was happening? Like sand through a sieve, these facts slowly filtered into his fractured mind. He frowned. A whole new set of problems surfaced. And he'd never been more shaky or vulnerable.

"Kira?" His voice was barely more than a croak.

"Thank God." She let out a very relieved sigh, her smile at once beautiful and reassuring. She pulled lightly at his tight grip, and he released her arms immediately. Her hands hovered for a moment, as if she didn't know quite what to do with them.

"Put them on me."

She stilled. Her gaze trapped in his. "What?"

"Your hands." His voice was gravelly, but he pushed on, knowing it was too late to do anything else. "Put them on me, Kira. Touch me."

Still she sat there, frozen, staring at him as if questioning whether he was experiencing another dream.

"Please," he whispered.

She choked on a sob; he could see the shiny tracks of her tears on her cheeks. Her body began to tremble as she slowly lowered her hands to his bare chest. He sucked in his breath as she let them skate lightly over him, leaning over to touch his face. His breath came out on a low groan when the soft fabric of her shorts rubbed against him.

She shuddered in response, her thighs and knees tightening against his sides as her body sought comfort.

The instant her fingers touched his lips, he surged into a raging erection. He clutched the sheets in order to keep from bucking against her, knowing if her muscles contracted against him, it would be over.

He kissed her fingertips, and she began to cry freely. She ran her fingers over the contours of his face. His eyes; cheeks; the thin scar on his forehead. Her touch was exquisite in its ability to heal as powerfully as it excited. Her stomach was pressed against his ribs now, her breasts brushing his chest, making his nipples harden almost painfully. "Put your mouth on me."

Her gaze shot to his. He almost pulled her into his arms then. The look in her eyes was beyond anything he'd ever experienced. He tightened further at the desire and excitement, felt blessed by the caring and concern. But there was something else, some inner light that fused the fractured gems into shining diamonds until they sparkled so brightly, he knew he'd die if she took it away.

"I want to," she whispered. "I've wanted to for a long time. Needed to. I . . . it's just . . . I can't seem to stop shaking."

"May I hold you?"

She didn't seem surprised by the request. He sensed she knew what he was really asking. He had given her the right to touch him. But he wouldn't touch her unless she did the same.

"Please."

He groaned, unable not to as he wrapped his arms around her and held her tightly against his chest. When she stretched out her legs along his, he rolled over, pulling her under him until she was tucked in the crook of his arm. He lifted his hand to touch her hair. "So beautiful."

Her lips parted, and he found it near impossible to resist the invitation. But there would be no hurrying this. He wanted each moment to stand apart from every other one. To carve every detail into his mind, to have something precious and good in his heart to go along with all the darkness and decay.

He traced her cheekbone, her lips, then her shoulder. Their eyes remained locked. His need to cherish fought with the need to be cherished. But she was here, beneath him. And it was a damn good start.

She slowly began unbuttoning her blouse. Her fingers were clumsy, but he let her do it alone, unable to move as he watched her. Light cotton gave way to pink silk. His fingers twitched against her shoulder, but otherwise he kept still. He throbbed against her thigh as she snapped the front clasp open. Well, most of him kept still.

Her breasts were perfection, softly rounded and as sun-kissed as the rest of her. He ached to take the dusky coral tips into his mouth. She didn't give him the chance.

Looking up at him, she deliberately put her palms on his chest and pushed gently. Her nails pressed against his flesh at his intake of breath. She kept pushing until he was on his back, and she leaned over him, flipping her hair over her shoulder so she could still look at his face.

Cole's breath lodged in his throat as she slowly let her eyes sweep down the length of his body. Her hands followed slowly, torturously.

"You're going to kill me, you know?"

The smile she turned on him was positively wicked. And as quickly as that, he felt the mood change. The tension hadn't diminished, had in fact been knocked up a giant notch. But it was as if they'd silently agreed to let go of all the questions and concerns that had led them to this point. For now they would simply revel in the wonder of discovering each other.

A slow grin curved his lips. He even began to chuckle when she shook her hair out in a dramatic flair while flinging her shirt off. His laugh ended on a choke as she slid her hands around him and began to stroke. "Dear Lord," he murmured, "there is a heaven."

She bent over, her lips poised just above him. "I hope so," she whispered. "You've seen enough of hell."

Before he could answer, she took him in her mouth. Any vestiges of the ghoulish nightmare he'd relived again and again over the past week evaporated in the hot wetness of her mouth. He took as much as he could, but by now he knew that this night could end only one way. If he was going to climax, then she would be right there with him.

"Kira." She didn't stop. He touched her hair. "Kira."

She finally released him, but he couldn't stop the sigh of disappointment that escaped his lips. She smiled.

"What?" She shifted her weight so she knelt beside him. Her hands never stopped touching him. She caressed, teased, even tickled.

He let her explore, let her strip away every barrier, reveling shamelessly in every second of it. When he thought he'd die from sensory overload, he said, "Take off your shorts."

She'd been massaging his calves, and his question apparently caught her off guard. She looked up at him for a moment, then said, "No."

Now she'd caught him off guard, but before he had time to recoup, she climbed on top of him and scooted up until the fly of her shorts was barely inches from his chin.

"You do it."

"Always the risk taker," he said with a lazy smile that barely curved his lips.

Kira trembled at the wicked gleam that entered his eyes. He gripped her hips, and suddenly she was on her back, and he was astride her thighs. His fingers were hot against the sensitive skin below her navel as he slid the button free and dragged the zipper down. He moved backward down the bed, pulling her shorts and bikinis off as he went.

Upright on his knees, he stared down at her, his grin now as deliciously wicked as the look in his eyes. He flung her shorts aside in the same dramatic fashion she'd discarded her shirt earlier. He was boldly magnificent; his skin, the same golden color everywhere, still glistened from his nocturnal battle. She'd dreamed so often of finally touching him that she was a bit awestruck at how far the reality had surpassed the fantasy.

It seemed as if she'd wanted him like this forever. Open and ready. Wanting her and willing to finally do something about it.

He bent and pressed the tip of his tongue on the inside of her calf. She arched instinctively, and he groaned in approval. "Grab the sheets, Kira," he murmured against the inside of her knee. "Hold on."

She was already clutching them. His tongue traced a slow, erotic path up along her thigh. "Cole, please."

He switched to light, teasing kisses. "Don't you believe in fair play?" He lifted his head slightly, looking straight at her as he added, "Sweet lips."

His tongue dipped into the curve between her legs, and she moaned. "Ohhh, yes." He continued his sweet assault until she was writhing against him. "Cole." Her voice was ragged, insistent.

He slid her legs from his shoulders and moved up between her thighs. "I will, sweetheart. But first I have to taste these."

He lowered his head and laved first one beaded nipple, then the other. It was exquisite. It was torture.

She wrapped her legs around his hips and pressed upward. He responded by pushing partly into her. When he stopped, she groaned loudly.

"I know, baby. But we can't—" He broke off as her muscles began to clench. "I have to . . ." His jaw twitched. "Protection," he managed to say through gritted teeth.

"The pill," she responded on a gasp, finally understanding. "It's okay."

"Thank God," he responded, and pushed fully into her.

Kira cried out in pleasure, her hands tight on his shoulders. They'd waited too long, pushed it too far to go slowly. Cole moved deeply inside of her. Her heels dug hard into his back as she matched him thrust for thrust. She buried her face in the center of his chest and moaned as he thrust harder, faster.

"Cole, Cole . . ." Her voice was ragged.

"Yeah, baby, I'm right here. Oh, Lord—" He broke off, groaning, as her nails scored his back.

Speech became impossible after that. The pace intensified until it became frenzied. Cole grunted and growled as he pushed into her. Over and over. He was primal, powerful. His scent, his sounds, his motions, drove her wild. He reduced her to her most basic need. And her need was him. All of him.

Pleasure coiled so tightly inside her, she felt spring-loaded. Peaking would be a violent whiplash of a ride she wasn't sure she could survive. She didn't care. She couldn't wait. But he kept on, harder and harder. Faster and faster. And she stayed with him. Civility was a pretense long forgotten. Wild and untamed, they were both fighting for breath. Fighting to get closer. Deeper.

And when he reached the very core, pushed beyond the point she could contain him, they both screamed in their release.

Kira clutched him as tightly as he held her, not letting go for the long minutes it took for the near-violent convulsions to slow to an erratic shuddering of muscles long spent.

When Cole could think straight, he rolled to his side and pulled her against him, her face against his throat, his buried in her hair. He lifted a trembling hand to push aside the damp strands clinging to her cheek. The curve of her neck was tantalizing, yet so slender and fragile. To look at her slim body, he could barely believe her capable of the near-animalistic mating that had just taken place.

"You okay?" he whispered when he could.

She tilted her head back to look at him, eyes shining, her lashes wet. "Oh yeah," she whispered back. "The very best I've ever been."

He grinned at her heartfelt answer. "You can say that again." She grinned back, but he could see the questions behind the smile. His stomach tightened. Not yet. He wasn't ready. He just wanted a few more hours. With her. Like this. "In the morning, Kira," he said softly.

She started to speak, but he pressed a finger against her lips, suddenly desperate to keep her here and not much caring how he did it. "Sleep with me. Keep the dreams away."

Her eyes softened, and she nestled almost instinctively against him, tugging his body around hers while wrapping herself around him. He should have felt like a bastard for playing on her need to care and nurture. But he didn't.

Probably because he'd meant every word.

He reached behind him to the floor for the sheet and drew it over them. She sighed as the slick material caressed her skin.

"Cole?" Her voice was sleepy soft.

He knew just how she felt. He tightened his hold on her. "Mmmm?"

She yawned. "White cotton and black satin?"

He understood. Unfortunately he wasn't about to explain. So he told her what he could. "I did some work for an emir once. He loved the stuff, had it everywhere. I sort of got used to it. Satin feels good, helps me sleep. But it's too slippery to lie on."

"Oh."

She didn't say anything after that, and eventually he felt her muscles relax as she drifted off into sleep.

Resting his head on hers, he shoved aside the rest of that story, especially the part about the emir having been one of the biggest dope dealers in the

Middle East. Instead, he thought about what had just happened between them.

But the ramifications of their actions were just as overwhelming, especially with the damp night air intoxicating him with the scent of her mingled with the scent of him. His body tightened, and he lay back slightly, folded her more closely against him. Twining his ankle around hers, he pulled her leg between his thighs. He stared down at her sleeping form. What was he going to do about her?

He squeezed his eyes shut as he pressed his lips against her hair. "And what are you going to do about me?"

Kira could have sworn it was crickets singing that woke her up. She forced her eyes open, but Cole had pulled the shutters over the windows earlier that morning, and the room was still cast in dark shadows. She smiled sleepily and flopped back on the pillows, forgetting about the crickets as she recalled how easily he'd persuaded her to pretend it wasn't morning yet. In fact, he'd successfully used that same argument twice. She was alone now, though, and she missed him.

"Cole?" No answer. She wasn't alarmed; he didn't *feel* gone. Not bothering to analyze that highly scientific response, she sat up, stretched, and pulled the sheet around her. He was right; satin did feel wonderful. And decadent. Sort of like its owner. She grinned and called to him again, a bit louder this time. Still no answer. "Okay," she muttered to herself, not really annoyed. She swung her legs over the bed and stood. Not finding anything immediately visible to wear—Lord knew where her clothes had ended up— she simply wrapped the satin sheet around her, toga style, and shuffled to the door.

She found him sitting at the bar. His back was to her. She was about to speak when she noticed what he held in his hand. *Damn.*

He pivoted in the chair until he faced her. She took her time before looking at his face. He was bare-chested, wearing only a faded pair of black gym shorts.

"You want to explain this?" His voice was low and even.

She looked at him. She couldn't exactly describe his expression, but he didn't look angry. "It's an envelope full of hundred-dollar bills."

"I can see that. Mind telling me what it's for?"

With a start she realized that what she saw was wariness. Cole Sinclair felt vulnerable. To her. She wanted to shout with joy. Except he didn't look as if he was enjoying this new facet of himself very much. Maintaining eye contact, she walked slowly toward him, not stopping until she was between his legs. Deliberately, she placed her hands on his shoulders, testing her theory. His muscles bunched under her fingers, and his jaw tightened, but otherwise he didn't move. Glory hallelujah, maybe she had a chance after all.

"Originally, it was my way of clearing the books between us. You helped me out, and I owed you. Simple business arrangement."

His eyes narrowed a bit. "And now?"

"And now I know it was an excuse, albeit a legitimate one," she added with a small smile.

He looked a bit less tense, but his shoulders were still tight under her light grip. "An excuse for what? You knew I wouldn't take it, didn't you? So why try?"

"Because I had to see you again."

His pupils expanded at her heartfelt answer. But his voice when he spoke was still guarded. "Then why come in the middle of the night? Normally, I wouldn't have been here."

"I didn't realize the truth until I saw your bike in the lot. Then I heard you shouting."

"Kira to the rescue," he said quietly. He broke eye contact, looking at the floor, shaking his head slightly. "I won't be another one of your charity cases."

She cupped his neck with her hand and placed her other hand on his shadowed cheek, lifting his head until their eyes met. "And I won't let you throw me away the way you apparently have everything else."

He studied her for a long moment, then said, "Where did you get it."

"What?"

He nodded at the envelope.

"Oh. The investors were very generous. Thanks to you. You deserve some of this, Cole."

"I don't want your damn money." His voice was hoarse.

"Fine!" She was yelling now, and she didn't care. This wasn't how it was supposed to go. He was pulling away from her again. Only this time she'd fight with everything she had. She snatched the envelope from his hand and tossed it on the floor behind her. "There. No longer an issue between us, okay?" She didn't wait for an answer. "Now I've answered your questions, you answer some of mine. Who's Felicia?"

He flinched at her less than diplomatic demand. "You don't pull any punches."

He looked at her, and she could see the battle waging behind his eyes. There was grief and fear, but most wrenching of all was the hopelessness she saw. "Tell me, Cole. You've got to get this . . . whatever it is that happened to you, out in the open."

"Don't play shrink with me, Kira," he warned. "I tried that two years ago. It didn't help then."

"Kiss me, Cole."

"What?" He looked at her as if she'd lost her last remaining marble.

She moved closer to him but didn't touch him. "I said, kiss me." When he continued to stare at her, she added, "You still want to, don't you?"

His eyebrows lifted a fraction, then lowered as he released a long breath. "Yeah, beats the hell out of fighting."

ELEVEN

Kira's lips had barely begun to curve in a smile when they were devoured by his. He clamped his hands on her hips and hauled her onto his lap. She wrapped her legs around his waist, holding him as tightly as he held her while pouring everything she felt, everything she had, into their kiss.

The second he broke off for air, she gulped some of her own and whispered, "Don't you see? I'm not trying to be a shrink, Cole. What's between us has nothing to do with the fact that you're hurting and I'm a trained healer." She gripped his head and held it tightly as she looked deeply into his eyes. "But it has everything to do with the fact that I love you." Her eyes burned at the brief flash of incredulous joy she saw in his, before his ingrained defenses shuttered them again. "And, dammit, if I want to help you, heal you, then it's because I want to have

a stake in the result. I want you in my life, Cole."
Tears tipped over her lashes and trickled down her
cheek. "I love you."

His eyes burned suspiciously bright at her fervent speech, but her vision blurred, and she simply
held on to him, waiting for him to say something,
anything.

"Felicia was my wife." His voice was a choked
whisper; his hands were still woven in her hair.

She stilled for a moment, then sniffed and reached
up to wipe her eyes. "What happened to her?"

He kept his gaze steady on hers, but they were
fierce now, openly filled with pain. "She was killed
when a bomb exploded on the boat I was using to
transport guns from Cuba to Miami." He paused,
scrutinizing her, apparently looking for whatever
response he seemed certain he'd find.

"And you survived. Oh, Cole, I'm so sorry. You
must have loved her very much." She could tell her
understanding wasn't the first response he'd expected.
"If you thought you'd put me off with the gunrunner
bit, you still don't believe me. I love you, Cole. I
don't care what you did, what you were."

"You don't care that because I was so involved
with my job, I let my wife and a dozen children
get blown to kingdom come?" His voice was brutal,
filled with self-loathing.

She flinched, unable to prevent the automatic
response to such a statement. Cole abruptly stood and

set her on her feet. He strode across the room, and she thought he meant to go on out the door, but before she could call him on running away, he stopped and turned back to her, eyes blazing.

"I should have known, Kira. I should have known she wouldn't give up her crusade to get those children out of Cuba."

He looked at once wild and beaten. But Kira didn't interrupt, didn't go to him. No matter how badly she wanted to help him through this, he needed to get it out in his own way.

"I was sent in to infiltrate a large cartel that was illegally transporting firearms into the States. Felicia was the sister of the cartel's top gun, Marcos. I was playing the sax in a little club outside of Havana, working my way into the ring as a runner. Marcos owned the club. He was my contact, my in. No one knew I was a plant. I'd been under for almost two years, gaining their trust, before we finally had everything in place. I hadn't counted on Felicia." He stopped and rubbed his palm over his eyes. "She was using her brother's connection to smuggle orphans out of Cuba."

"She knew what he really did for a living?"

"Yeah. She hated it, but she also knew she couldn't change it. Marcos was devoted to her, and as long as she made sure no one knew what she was doing, he looked the other way. She was always very cautious."

"You helped her, didn't you? She smuggled them out on your runs." It wasn't really a question, but he nodded.

"I was . . . I don't know, captivated by her, I guess. I was so far away from everything normal, so entrenched in my role, and she represented a niche of sanity, of goodness, in the middle of all the filth and evil."

"What happened? Did she know who you really were?"

"No." The word was bitten off, an oath. "She knew I was an American citizen, but she believed I worked for her brother."

Kira's smile was small and ironic. "And she loved you anyway."

Cole bowed his head. "I shouldn't have lied to her. I guess part of me knew the loyalty between brother and sister went both ways. She might have turned me in. I couldn't allow that to happen."

Kira shook her head slowly, wondering if Felicia would have turned him in. Wondering what she'd do in the same situation. Her family ties were pretty strong, too, but she simply couldn't imagine betraying Cole.

"I knew things were about to hit the fan," he continued, "and I wanted her safe. The only way I could do that was to marry her and get her the hell out of there. I set her up in an apartment in Miami. I saw her when I was on this side. But I knew it was all going to go down soon. I figured we'd pull off the sting, and I'd quit and come back to her. I'd tell her everything. If she was still willing after I got done, then I'd have done everything in my power to make it work."

"What happened?"

Abruptly he turned away, placing his palms flat on the wall next to the glass door. Suddenly she didn't want to put him through the last part. Didn't want him to relive it again, fully conscious and wide open for the pain.

"Never mind," she said quickly, crossing the room toward him. He didn't turn, and she stopped a foot away from his broad back. "It's enough that I know you feel responsible. But I also know that whatever happened wasn't—couldn't have been—your fault. Not deliberately. I know you."

He whirled around, tears standing on the edge of his black lashes. He clenched his fists at his side. "I left her in Miami. My thoughts totally on my mission. She got a job in a small Cuban grocery; she made friends. She seemed happy, content. Not once did I think that she'd find some way to continue her efforts. In Miami, of all places. She was smart and resourceful. She made contacts and was bold enough, sure enough, to push things until she got them set up."

"But she didn't tell you?"

"No—"

"Well, then how can you take the blame?"

"Because I should have known!" he roared. "She was my wife!" He grabbed her shoulders as if he meant to shake her, but he didn't; he just held her. "She used my boat that night. The night the raid was taking place. She couldn't have known what was going to happen. I had no idea she was aboard. Things didn't go smoothly. Marcos figured out who I was and launched a bomb at my boat just as the other agents were closing in." He shut his eyes tightly for a moment.

"Cole, don't—"

They flashed open. "It missed. I tried to move away, draw him after me so the rest of the operation wouldn't fall apart. But just then this blur rushes past me and dives into the water. Then Felicia storms out of the below-deck hatch after him. It threw me, but she was yelling at me to save him, and I didn't have the time to think. I turned and saw the young boy swimming as fast as he could away from the boat. Another round of bullets blew the side of the boat to hell, killing the motor. I shoved Felicia down, shouted to Marcos that his sister was on the boat, then dove into the water after the boy."

Cole's eyes were glazed with pain, his expression tortured. Kira moved closer to him, running a soothing touch over his cheek. She knew he was in the clutches of the nightmare and wouldn't stop until he'd finished, but she couldn't stand there and do nothing. She wished she'd never forced this on him.

"The boy must have panicked when he heard the shots," he went on doggedly, sweat beading on his forehead and temples. "It took a while for me to catch up to him. We'd just turned back when it happened." He began to shake. "Marcos hadn't heard me, or he'd never have done it. Another bomb, Kira," he whispered, his voice ragged with grief. "Only it didn't miss. I couldn't get to them. I was too far out. They . . . they—"

His voice broke and Kira pulled him into her arms. His arms went around her so tightly her breath was cut off. She didn't mind. She was crying freely now, and from the racking motion of his chest and shoulders, she suspected he was too. "I love you," she whispered through the tears. She didn't bother telling him it wasn't his fault. She told him what he needed to hear now. This she could—had to—make him know and believe. "I love you, Cole Sinclair."

He just held her. She had no idea how long they stood there, didn't care. Finally, he pushed his face into the hair tangled at the side of her neck. He nuzzled through and placed a soft, heartbreakingly sweet kiss below her ear where her skin pulsed. "Then it's wasted, Kira. Don't love me."

She pulled her head back and held his face between her hands until he looked at her. She wanted to cry all over again at what she saw there.

Added to the pain and despair, she saw defeat. No! "Too late for that," she said softly. "Cole, if you had been killed during the raid, would you expect Felicia to take the blame? After all, she had to know you were under a constant threat of danger, yet she put you at deliberate risk by not telling you she'd stowed herself and the children aboard. You said she was smart and resourceful. You even suspected she might turn you in. Maybe she had her own agenda all along. No one will ever know. But the bottom line was, she was an adult, and it was her actions that placed those children at risk—not yours."

"That's just it, Kira. My whole life—hers too—was about playing roles. Playing one person against another to get the job done."

"But you were one of the good guys!"

He laughed, but it was empty of humor. He stalked over to the opposite wall, slamming his hand so hard against it that she jumped. "See these?" He ran his fingers over the scattered holes she'd noticed her first night aboard. "Bullet holes, Kira." He swung his arm in a wide arc, encompassing the room's furnishings. "You know how I got this boat? It was picked up during a drug raid. I got it real cheap because it was too beat-up to salvage for auction. Lord only knows what went on in this very room, but did I care? No, it was a job perk to me."

He walked back to her, standing so close, she could feel the vibrations of his voice on her skin.

"It's not just what happened that night. It was all of it. I ran guns, for God's sake! Just because I was going to get them in the end, or planned to, doesn't make it any easier to live with. It eats away at you, Kira, until you're no longer sure who's on the good side, or even if there is one. After that night, I got out. I knew I'd never be able to function in that world again. Problem was, I couldn't function anywhere else, either." He voice was ragged, his grip on her shoulders too tight. He took a deep breath. "If I can't learn to live with myself, Kira," he said quietly, "then how the hell do you expect me to live with you?"

Kira swore she could feel her heart splinter apart. The ache in her chest escalated to a clutching pain as he let his hands drop and took a step back away from her.

Her skin cooled immediately with the removal of his body heat. She was only vaguely dismayed to discover she was standing in front of him stark naked, the satin sheet having fallen off long ago.

She turned and sought the sheet, not because she had a sudden attack of modesty, but because it gave her something to do. A small step toward leaving him. If she concentrated very hard, she could take another one, then another. . . .

She made it as far as his bedroom door when her steps faltered. The silence was deafening. The numbness began to fade when she was faced with a harsh choice. To get her clothes, she had to go into the bedroom. His bedroom. A place she'd left not long ago filled with dreams and warmth and naive plans for her future. Their future.

But her other option was to turn and face him again. She wasn't ready for that either. And suddenly she was angry. At herself for getting into this predicament, at Cole for not being willing to fight for what she knew—*knew*—they could have together. Now it seemed imperative to get the hell out of there before she did something even more foolish. Like begging him, or pleading with him.

But to do that she needed her clothes. Closing her mind to the tantalizing visions of last night and this morning, she stormed into his bedroom and flung the bedclothes around until she found everything. She yanked them on and left the satin sheet where it had dropped. She took a moment to gather herself; then, realizing that might take years, she stepped back out into the living room.

He was still standing by the glass doors. He was only twenty or so feet away from her, but he might as well have been twenty miles away. His expression . . . wasn't. His face was closed. Remote and distant. She looked away, then walked directly to where the envelope had fallen. The money had spilled out onto the carpet, and she carefully gathered it and tucked it back inside. Then she stood and moved to the bar, laid it down, then turned to face him. His gaze was riveted on hers, but his expression hadn't changed. She started toward the opposite door.

"Take it," she heard him say.

She paused, but only for a second. She flipped the latch and slid the door open just enough for her to fit through. She was halfway out when she stopped. She bowed her head, a sigh escaping her lips. Apparently she was going to have to face that he'd been right about one thing. She had absolutely no sense of self-protection.

She stepped back inside but kept one hand on the door. "The money is yours, Cole. Like I said earlier, it's a business transaction. You can burn it for all I care, but I won't take it back. Now we have no obligations between us." She took a breath. The next part was the hardest. Probably the most difficult thing she would ever do. And possibly the most painful. She walked across the room, praying silently, repeatedly, that he would let her get through it.

She stopped with barely a breath of air between them. He might as well have been made of granite. He didn't so much as blink when she laid her hand against his cheek. Lifting up on tiptoe, she kissed him on the lips, breaking away quickly without giving him time to respond. His arms were still at his side. His expression had finally changed, but the bleak hollowness she saw didn't encourage her a bit.

She took a step back. "You let me touch you,

Cole. I know you want me to." She walked to the glass doors and wrenched open the vertical blinds. "I want to see you in the sun. I want to touch you. I need you. I love you. Fight for me, Cole," she repeated, "like I'm fighting for you right now." She moved back to the doorway, her courage rapidly dwindling in the face of his continued silence. She looked back at him. "If you do, I promise you'll never regret it. But do it soon, Cole, because I won't wait around for you forever."

She rushed out then, leaping to the dock, stumbling, then righting herself. She ran toward the end of the pier, knowing she'd lied about one thing. She would wait for him. Forever, if necessary.

The sound of shattering glass pierced the quiet with a sudden violence, and Kira skidded to stop. She started to turn back but didn't. There was nothing else she could do for him. Whatever happened next, if anything did, would have to come from him.

All she could do was wait. And love him.

Kira held the cold glass of iced tea against her forehead, then moved it down to the open throat of her shirt. She tilted her head back and let the sun beat down mercilessly on her closed eyelids while the moisture from the glass trickled soothingly between her breasts.

The gunning of a motorcycle engine made her

start, but she refused to take the bait. It had been almost a month since she'd walked out of Cole's life, and it was long past time to stop jumping up every time a bike roared by. The sound faded, and she turned back to her garden.

Heaving a sigh, she spared a glance at her weathered house, then knelt by one of the massive pilings that kept her house aloft and hopefully safe from hurricanes. Several cars and what sounded like a truck lumbered down the road out in front, but she ignored the intrusion into her day off. She'd just speared her trowel into the dirt when a shadow fell across her. She looked up, expecting a neighbor or lost tourist. She literally fell back onto the sandy grass when she saw who was looking down at her.

Cole reached a hand down to lift her up, but she was so shocked—and not too certain he wasn't a mirage compounded from desperation and too much sun—that she simply sat there. After a minute he dropped his hand, then sat in the grass next to her.

"Hello, Kira."

Now it was her turn to be wary and guarded. "Cole." It was all she could say. He stared at her in a way that could only be described as hungry. But his casual position, knees bent with his arms resting on them, belied that look. So she didn't let herself trust it. She only hoped she wasn't looking at him the same way.

Finally, when the silence became uncomfortable,

she asked, "Why are you here?" His throat bobbed as he swallowed visibly. Cole nervous?

"I've been talking with Reese."

Her eyes widened. "Reese?" She didn't know what she'd expected him to say, but it wasn't that.

"Yeah. He told me to tell you that Juan Carlos's wife, Magdalene, has begun to seek help for their son. I guess with her husband facing a long prison term, she's been able to take some control. He thought you might want to know, you know . . . in case . . ." His voice faded away as the look in his eyes heated up.

There was no doubt now. He was hungry . . . and nervous. "Is that why you're here? To pass on a message from Reese?"

He waited for an excruciatingly long time before answering. "No." He stood up abruptly and reached for her hand again. "I want to show you something. Come with me?"

She didn't answer, but she held up her hand. The contact of palm to fingers was like putting a match to a stick of dynamite. He pulled her up easily, until she stood only a few inches away. He looked as if he wanted to say something, but he turned and headed for the front of the house. She followed beside him. They rounded the house, and she saw a huge, shiny black pickup in the driveway. In the back, held with cross ties and surrounded by some packing boxes, was his bike.

"Yours?" She nodded toward the truck.

He shook his head. "Reese's."

He walked to the side of the truck, then turned to face her. She noticed his sax case and another large box with holes punched in it on the passenger seat. She remembered the box from his bedroom. It had been in the corner. But she was too curious by the entire setup to question it. She turned back to him, waiting for him to speak.

"You told me you loved me," he began quietly, his gaze not quite meeting hers. "And you wanted me to fight for you." His voice, fine moments ago, now wavered a bit. "In one morning you handed me my most desired wish and the toughest assignment I've ever been given. I thought I could handle you, Kira. But I think I was lost from the moment you walked into Repo's bar." He looked away for a moment, squinting against the bright sun. "After the explosion, I'd retreated into a dark hole to lick my wounds. Only somehow I never managed to crawl back out." He looked at her. "I think now that maybe it was because I didn't have a reason. I'd like to say I was man enough to come to terms with my life, my past and my future, on my own. But the truth of it is, I didn't have the strength or enough of a belief in myself to do it."

He studied her for a moment. "Not like you did. You came waltzing into my life and made me feel things . . . you made me want. I'd spent two years making damn sure I'd never want anything again. But I wanted you. I wanted you so badly, I burned with it. It scared the living hell out of me."

"Cole—"

He held up his hand, but she reached up anyway and wiped away the tears from his cheeks with her thumb. He stepped closer and returned the gesture. She hadn't been aware until that moment that she'd begun to cry.

He kept his thumbs on her cheeks, his hand cupping her face. "Then," he said, trying to smile, but his voice choked, "just when I think I've been able to walk away, to let you go, you come storming onto my boat, throwing money at me and telling me you love me. And you did love me, scars and all. It blew me away. You gave me something no one else ever has. Your heart. Your whole heart. And all you asked of me was that I give the same care to yours that you were willing to give to mine." His voice tightened. "It was the very least you deserved. And I wanted to take it, Kira. But it seemed as if that was all I was capable of. Taking from you. You seemed to think I had something to give back. Only, I knew that wasn't true. Until you left."

"And then?" she whispered tremulously.

"And then I knew I'd already given you the only thing I had. My heart." He let his hands drop away and turned to face the bed of his truck. "But it wasn't much of a gift at that point. You left me with a huge challenge. But you also left me with one hell of a motivation to achieve it." He turned back to face her. Taking a deep breath, he said, "I sold my boat. I sent the money from that along with what you gave me to the refugee center for children in Miami that Felicia dealt with. I'd already been doing some minor security work for Sandy and Repo, so I put out the word that I was thinking about going into business. Reese contacted me and surprised me by offering a partnership of sorts. Seems he's ready to toss in the federal towel, too." He stepped closer to her. He tilted her chin up with one rough-tipped finger until their eyes met.

"I'm standing here with everything I own. My past is over. I have no present. I have only a future. I want to share it with you. On whatever terms you'll take me. I love you, Kira. With my whole heart."

Kira knew she'd be able to recall that moment in perfect detail for the rest of her life: Cole, standing proudly before her, laying his heart at her feet. The sun backlighting his dark good looks with an intensity that moonlight and shadows could never hope to match. But most of all, she'd remember his eyes. Once they'd been windows to the darkness that shadowed his soul. Now the walls were gone, the barriers he'd painfully erected shattered. There for her to see was all the pain, fear, and vulnerability that were the legacy of his past. But along with them now was fierce pride. And an emotion so powerful, she was almost afraid to believe it was all for her.

But it was. And it was love.

And she vowed, then and there, that she would give this man the very best that was her, love him with every breath that she took.

A warmth stole through her. Because she knew he would love her with every breath he took. But what made her heart fill, along with her eyes, was the realization that she already had the very best of him. She had his love.

She flung herself into his arms, and Cole locked them around her back, swinging her around and around. He finally set her down and kissed her. When he could, he pulled his lips from hers. "Is that a yes?"

She was grinning so widely, she could hardly speak. "That is a big, resounding yes. I love you, Cole Sinclair."

"Lord, I've needed to hear that. I know it won't be easy—"

"Yeah, you're going into business with Reese," she said, her smile tempering the sarcasm in her tone.

"Kira, I'll do whatever it takes, but I promise you'll never regret loving me."

Kira's eyes teared up again, and she laughed joyfully at his echo of her parting words a month—and a lifetime—ago. "Are we going to stand out here all day, or can we go inside and start working on that future you mentioned?" Her voice was teasing, and she traced a fingernail around the rim of his ear.

He growled, then scooped her up in his arms and headed for the house. A scuffling sound from the front seat of his truck stopped him.

"Cole?"

"Uh, Kira? There's one other thing we need to discuss."

"If you mean the 'terms' you spoke of, then I'll let you know right now, I'll put up with your chauvinistic Australian buddy, but be warned, I'm going to lobby real hard for an incredibly sexy white dress and a big gooey wedding cake."

That earned her a down-to-her-soles, mind-blowing kiss. "Absolutely, sweet lips. But that wasn't what I was referring to." Glancing over her shoulder into the cab of his truck, he set her down gently and walked around to the passenger-side door, drawing her along with him. He turned to face her, and she wanted to laugh at the honest concern in his eyes.

"Cole, whatever it is, it can't be worth worrying over."

"You might want to hold judgment on that. You ever heard of the saying Love me, love my dog, or cat, or whatever?"

Thoroughly confused, she went along with him anyway. "Yeah, sure."

"Well, I think I've got one you've never heard."

He reached in and flipped the lid off the large box. "How about love me, love my iguana?"

Kira peered into the box then looked back at Cole in complete shock. "Elvis?"

"In the scaly flesh."

"But I thought you said Axe cooked him."

"No, I said I gave him to Axe to hide. Axe dumped him on me, said he didn't want to be the one to give him to Iggy, figured Iggy wasn't going to be real reasonable about it. Then you and I got caught up, and I didn't have a chance to get him back down to Repo's."

"You had him all along?" She remembered waking up to crickets the morning after they'd made love and recalled just where that box had been. "He was in the bedroom with us?"

"Well, I didn't exactly have a chance to move him."

"I can't believe I never knew he was there."

Cole shrugged, the defensive expression on his face completely endearing. "I guess I have a natural talent at hiding iguanas."

A smile curved her lips. "I'm surprised a big bad guy like you didn't just turn him loose."

Cole actually colored. "I tried that. He came back."

Kira laughed. "Well, you know Iggy has a reward for him, just take him back. By now he won't care that you stole him in the first place."

"I didn't steal him. Not really." He seemed to redden a bit further, then muttered something she couldn't quite hear.

"What was that?"

"I said I already tried to give him back. Apparently Iggy has acquired a new pet. A ten-foot-long boa constrictor. He's asking everyone to call him Snake now."

Kira put a fist to her mouth, but couldn't stifle the giggle. "He'll need a new neck tattoo. What did he name the thing? Wait a minute, don't tell me. Elvis Two."

Cole finally cracked a grin, the confession finally over. "Worse. It's a she. Iggy, or Snake, I guess, thinks it's the reincarnation of Marilyn Monroe."

"He named a ten-foot python—"

"Boa."

"Whatever! He named it Marilyn?"

"Yep." He shifted his weight for a moment, then turned and replaced the lid.

"Will he be all right in there for a while?"

"Should be, why?"

"Now that I've seen our pet—which you will feed and keep away from my face at all costs—"

His grin was devilish as he stepped toward her. "If I promise you'll never have to touch—or taste— a cricket, can we go inside?"

"I thought you'd never ask."

He pulled her into his arms for a kiss that bordered on public indecency, then swept her up and literally raced up the front steps. Once inside, he stopped, taking a moment to adjust to the dimmer light. "Where is your room?" he whispered against her lips as he kissed her again.

Minutes later, when she managed to drag her mouth from his, she answered, "Our room. And it's upstairs. You'll know it when you see it."

He carried her up the short flight, covering her face and neck with hot, wild kisses. For her part, she couldn't keep her hands—or mouth—off of him either.

Cole found the room immediately, a grin spreading across his face. "Ah, sweet lips, you have been waiting for me." He let her slide down onto the bed. "You know how I feel about satin sheets, sweetheart. But red?"

Kira smiled a bit wickedly as she pulled off her shirt. "Yeah, but wait until you see the matching underwear."

THE EDITOR'S CORNER

The coming month brings to mind lions and lambs—not only because of the weather but also because of our six wonderful LOVESWEPTs. In these books you'll find fierce and feisty, warm and gentle characters who add up to a rich and exciting array of people whose stories of falling in love are enthralling.

Judy Gill starts things off this month with another terrific story in **KISS AND MAKE UP**, LOVESWEPT #678. He'd never been around when they were married, but now that Kat Waddell has decided to hire a nanny to help with the kids, her ex-husband, Rand, insists he's perfect for the job! Accepting his offer means letting him live in the basement apartment—too dangerously close for a man whose presence arouses potent memories of reckless passion . . . and painful images of love gone wrong. He married Kat hoping for the perfect fantasy family, but the pretty picture he'd imagined didn't include an unhappy wife he never seemed to satisfy . . . except in bed. Now Rand needs to show Kat he's changed. The sensual magic he weaves makes her feel cherished at last, but Kat wonders if it's enough to mend their broken vows. Judy's special touch makes this story of love reborn especially poignant.

It's on to Scotland for **LORD OF THE ISLAND,** LOVESWEPT #679, by the wonderfully talented Kimberli Wagner. Ian MacLeod is annoyed by the American woman who comes to stay on Skye during the difficult winter months, but when Tess Hartley sheds her raingear, the laird is enchanted by the dark-eyed siren whose fiery temper reveals a rebel who won't be ordered around by any man—even him! He expects pity, even revulsion at the evidence of his terrible accident, but Tess's pain runs as deep as his does, and her artist's eye responds to Ian's scarred face with wonder at his courage . . . and a wildfire hunger to lose herself in his arms. As always, Kimberli weaves an intense story of love and triumph you won't soon forget.

Victoria Leigh gives us a hero who is rough, rugged, and capable of **DANGEROUS LOVE,** LOVESWEPT #680. Four years earlier, he'd fallen in love with her picture, but when Luke Sinclair arrives on her secluded island to protect his boss's sister from the man who'd once kidnapped her, he is stunned to find that Elisabeth Connor is more exquisite than he'd dreamed—and not nearly as fragile as he'd feared. Instead, she warms to the fierce heat of his gaze, begging to know the ecstacy of his touch. Even though he's sworn to protect her with his life, Elisabeth must make him see that she wants him to share it with her instead. Only Victoria could deliver a romance that's as sexy and fun as it is touching.

We're delighted to have another fabulous book from Laura Taylor this month, and **WINTER HEART,** LOVESWEPT #681, is Laura at her best. Suspicious that the elegant blonde has a hidden agenda when she hires him to restore a family mansion, Jack McMillan quickly puts Mariah Chandler on the defensive—and is shocked to feel a flash flood of heat and desire rush through him! He believes she is only a spoiled rich girl indulging a whim, but he can't deny the hunger that ignites within him to possess her. Tantalized by sensual longings she's never expected to feel, Mariah surrenders to the dizzying pleasure of Jack's embrace. She's fought her demons by helping other women who have suffered but has never told Jack of the shadows that still haunt her nights. Now Mariah must heal his wounded spirit by finally sharing her pain and daring him to share a future.

Debra Dixon brings together a hot, take-charge Cajun and a sizzling TV seductress in **MIDNIGHT HOUR,** LOVESWEPT #682. Her voice grabs his soul and turns him inside out before he even sees her, but when Dr. Nick Devereaux gazes at Midnight Mercy Malone, the town's TV horror-movie hostess, he aches to muss her gorgeous russet hair . . . and make love to the lady until she moans his name! Still, he likes her even better out of her slinky costumes, an everyday enchantress who tempts him to make regular house calls. His sexy accent gives her goosebumps, but Mercy hopes her lusty alter ego might scare off a man she fears will choose work over her. Yet, his kisses send her up in flames and make her ache for love that never ends. Debra's spectacular romance will leave you breathless.

Olivia Rupprecht invites you to a **SHOTGUN WEDDING,** LOVESWEPT #683. Aaron Breedlove once fled his mountain hamlet to escape his desire for Addy McDonald, but now fate has brought him back— and his father's deathbed plea has given him no choice but to keep the peace between the clans and marry his dangerous obsession! With hair as dark as a moonlit night, Addy smells of wildflowers and rainwater, and Aaron can deny his anguished passion no longer. He is the knight in shining armor she's always dreamed of, but Addy yearns to become his wife in every way—and

Aaron refuses to accept her gift or surrender his soul.
SHOTGUN WEDDING is a sensual, steamy romance
that Olivia does like no one else.

Happy reading,

With warmest wishes,

Nita Taublib

Nita Taublib

Associate Publisher

P.S. Don't miss the spectacular women's novels coming
from Bantam in April: **DARK PARADISE** is the dangerously erotic novel of romantic suspense from nationally bestselling author Tami Hoag; **WARRIOR BRIDE**
is a sizzling medieval romance in the bestselling tra-
dition of Julie Garwood from Tamara Leigh, a daz-
zling new author; **REBEL IN SILK** is the fabulous new
Once Upon a Time romance from bestselling Loveswept
author Sandra Chastain. We'll be giving you a sneak peek
at these terrific books in next month's LOVESWEPTs.
And immediately following this page, look for a preview
of the spectacular women's fiction books from Bantam
available now!

Don't miss these exciting books by your
favorite Bantam authors

On sale in February:
*SILK AND
STONE*
by Deborah Smith

*LADY
DANGEROUS*
by Suzanne Robinson

*SINS OF
INNOCENCE*
by Jean Stone

Deborah Smith

SILK AND STONE

From Miracle *to* Blue Willow, *Deborah Smith's evocative novels have won a special place in readers' hearts. Now comes a spellbinding, unforgettably romantic new work. Vibrant with wit, aching with universal emotion, SILK AND STONE is Deborah Smith at her most triumphant . . .*

She had everything ready for him, everything but herself. What could she say to a husband she hadn't seen or spoken to in ten years: *Hi, honey, how'd your decade go?*

The humor was nervous, and morbid. She knew that. Samantha Raincrow hurt for him, hurt in ways she couldn't put into words. Ten years of waiting, of thinking about what he was going through, of *why* he'd been subjected to it, had worn her down to bare steel.

What he'd endured would always be her fault.

She moved restlessly around the finest hotel suite in the city, obsessed with straightening fresh flowers that were already perfectly arranged in their vases. He wouldn't have seen many flowers. She wanted him to remember the scent of youth and freedom. Of love.

Broad windows looked out over Raleigh. A nice city for a reunion. The North Carolina summer had just begun; the trees still wore the dark shades of new spring leaves.

She wanted everything to be new for him, but knew it could never be, that they were both haunted by the past—betrayals that couldn't be undone. She was Alexandra Lomax's niece; she couldn't scrub that stain out of her blood.

Her gifts were arranged around the suite's sitting room; Sam went to them and ran her hands over each one. A silk tapestry, six-feet-square and woven in geometrics from an old Cherokee design, was draped over a chair. She wanted him to see one of the ways she'd spent all the hours alone. Lined up in a precise row along one wall were five large boxes filled with letters she'd written to him and never sent, because he wouldn't have read them. A journal of every day. On a desk in front of the windows were stacks of bulging photo albums. One was filled with snapshots of her small apartment in California, the car she'd bought second-hand, years ago, and still drove, more of her tapestries, and her loom. And the Cove. Pictures of the wild Cove, and the big log house where he'd been born. She wanted him to see how lovingly she'd cared for it over the years.

The other albums were filled with her modeling portfolio. A strange one, by most standards. Just hands. Her hands, the only beautiful thing about her, holding soaps and perfumes and jewelry, caressing lingerie and detergent and denture cleaner, and a thousand other products. Because she wanted him to understand everything about her work, she'd brought the DeMeda book, too—page after over-sized, sensual page of black-and-white art photos. Photos of her fingertips touching a man's glistening, naked back, or molded to the crest of a muscular, bare thigh.

If he cared, she would explain about the ludicrous amount of money she'd gotten for that work, and that the book had been created by a famous photographer, and was considered an art form. If he cared, she'd assure him that there was nothing provocative about standing under hot studio lights with her hands cramping, while beautiful, half-clothed male models yawned and told her about their latest boyfriends.

If he cared.

Last, she went to a small, rectangular folder on a coffee table near the room's sofa. She sat down and opened it, her hands shaking so badly she could barely grasp the folder. The new deed for the Cove, with both his name and hers on it, was neatly tucked inside. She'd promised to transfer title to him the day he came home. If she hadn't held her ownership of the Cove over him like a threat all these years, he would have divorced her.

She hadn't promised to let him have it without her.

Sam hated that coercion, and knew he hated it, too. It was too much like something her Aunt Alexandra would have done. But Sam would not lose him, not without fighting for a second chance.

The phone rang. She jumped up, scattering the paperwork on the carpet, and ran to answer. "Dreyfus delivery service," said a smooth, elegantly drawling voice. "I have one slightly-used husband for you, ma'am."

Their lawyer's black sense of humor didn't help matters. Her heart pounded, and she felt dizzy. "Ben, you're downstairs?"

"Yes, in the lobby. Actually, I'm in the lobby. He's in the men's room, changing clothes."

"*Changing clothes?*"

"He asked me to stop on the way here. I perform many functions, Sam, but helping my clients pick a new outfit is a first."

"Why in the world—"

"He didn't want you to see him in what they gave him to wear. In a manner of speaking, he wanted to look like a civilian, again."

Sam inhaled raggedly and bowed her head, pressing her fingertips under her eyes, pushing hard. She wouldn't cry, wouldn't let him see her for the first time in ten years with her face swollen and her nose running. Small dignities were all she had left. "Has he said anything?" she asked, when she could trust herself to speak calmly.

"Hmmm, lawyer-client confidentiality, Sam. I represent both of you. What kind of lawyer do you think I am? Never mind, I don't want to hear the brutal truth."

"One who's become a good friend."

Ben hesitated. "Idle flattery." Then, slowly, "He said he would walk away without ever seeing you, again, if he could."

She gripped the phone numbly. *That's no worse than you expected*, she told herself. But she felt dead inside. "Tell him the doors to the suite will be open."

"All right. I'm sure he needs all the open doors he can get."

"I can't leave them all open. If I did, I'd lose him." Ben didn't ask what she meant; he'd helped her engineer some of those closed doors.

"Parole is not freedom," Ben said. "He understands that."

"And I'm sure he's thrilled that he's being forced to live with a wife he doesn't want."

"I suspect he doesn't know what he wants, at the moment."

"He's always known, Ben. That's the problem."

She said good-bye, put the phone down and walked with leaden resolve to the suite's double doors. She opened them and stepped back. For a moment, she considered checking herself in a mirror one last time, turned halfway, then realized she was operating on the assumption that what she looked like mattered to him. So she faced the doors and waited.

Each faint whir and rumble of the elevators down the hall made her nerves dance. She could barely breathe, listening for the sound of those doors opening. She smoothed her upswept hair, then anxiously fingered a blond strand that had escaped. Jerking at each hair, she pulled them out. A dozen or more, each unwilling to go. If it hurt, she didn't notice.

She clasped her hands in front of her pale yellow suitdress, then unclasped them, fiddled with the gold braid along the neck, twisted the plain gold wedding band on her left hand. She never completely removed it from her body, even when she worked. It had either remained on her finger or on a sturdy gold chain around her neck, all these years.

That chain, lying coldly between her breasts, also held his wedding ring.

She heard the hydraulic purr of an elevator settling into place, then the softer rush of metal doors sliding apart. Ten years compressed in the nerve-wracking space of a few seconds. If he weren't the one walking up the long hall right now, if some unsuspecting stranger strolled by instead, she thought her shaking legs would collapse.

Damn the thick carpeting. She couldn't gauge his steps. She wasn't ready. No, she would always be ready. Her life stopped, and she was waiting, waiting . . .

He walked into the doorway and halted. This tall, broad-shouldered stranger was her husband. Every memory she had of his appearance was there, stamped with a brutal decade of maturity, but there. Except for the look in his eyes. Nothing had ever been bleak and hard about him before. He stared at her with an intensity that could have burned her shadow on the floor.

Words were hopeless, but all that they had. "Welcome back," she said. Then, brokenly, *"Jake."*

He took a deep breath, as if a shiver had run through him. He closed the doors without ever taking his eyes off her. Then he was at her in two long steps, grasping her by the shoulders, lifting her to her toes. They were close enough to share a breath, a heartbeat. "I trained myself not to think about you," he said, his voice a raw whisper. "Because if I had, I would have lost my mind."

"I never deserted you. I wanted to be part of your life, but you wouldn't let me. Will you please try now?"

"Do you still have it?" he asked.

Anger. Defeat. The hoarse sound she made contained both. "Yes."

He released her. "Good. That's all that matters."

Sam turned away, tears coming helplessly. After all these years, there was still only one thing he wanted from her, and it was the one thing she hated, a symbol of pride and obsession she would never understand, a blood-red stone that had controlled the lives of too many people already, including theirs.

The Pandora ruby.

LADY DANGEROUS
by
Suzanne Robinson

*"An author with star quality . . . spectacularly
talented."*
—Romantic Times

*Liza Elliot had a very good reason for posing as a
maid in the house of the notorious Viscount Radcliffe.
It was the only way the daring beauty could discover
whether this sinister nobleman had been responsible for
her brother's murder. But Liza never knew how much
she risked until the night she came face-to-face with the
dangerously arresting and savagely handsome viscount
himself . . .*

Iron squealed against iron as the footmen swung
the gates back again. Black horses trotted into view,
two pairs, drawing a black lacquered carriage. Liza
stirred uneasily as she realized that vehicle, tack,
and coachman were all in unrelieved black. Pol-
ished brass lanterns and fittings provided the only
contrast.

The carriage pulled up before the house, the
horses stamping and snorting in the cold. The
coachman, wrapped in a driving coat and muffled in
a black scarf, made no sound as he controlled the ill-
tempered menace of his animals. She couldn't help

leaning forward a bit, in spite of her growing trepidation. Perhaps it was the eeriness of the fog-drenched night, or the unnerving appearance of the shining black and silent carriage, but no one moved.

Then she saw it. A boot. A black boot unlike any she'd ever seen. High of heel, tapered in the toe, scuffed, and sticking out of the carriage window. Its owner must be reclining inside. As she closed her mouth, which had fallen open, Liza saw a puff of smoke billow out from the interior. So aghast was she at this unorthodox arrival, she didn't hear the duke and his brother come down the steps to stand near her.

Suddenly the boot was withdrawn. The head footman immediately jumped forward and opened the carriage door. The interior lamps hadn't been lit. From the darkness stepped a man so tall, he had to curl almost double to keep his hat from hitting the roof of the vehicle.

The footman retreated as the man straightened. Liza sucked in her breath, and a feeling of unreality swamped her other emotions. The man who stood before her wore clothing so dark, he seemed a part of the night and the gloom of the carriage that had borne him. A low-crowned hat with a wide brim concealed his face, and he wore a long coat that flared away from his body. It was open, and he brushed one edge of it back where it revealed buckskin pants, a vest, a black, low-slung belt and holster bearing a gleaming revolver.

He paused, undisturbed by the shock he'd created. Liza suddenly remembered a pamphlet she'd seen on the American West. That's where she'd seen a man like this. Not anywhere in England, but in illustrations of the American badlands.

At last the man moved. He struck a match on his belt and lit a thin cigar. The tip glowed, and for a moment his face was revealed in the light of the match. She glimpsed black, black hair, so dark it seemed to absorb the flame of the match. Thick lashes lifted to reveal the glitter of cat-green eyes, a straight nose, and a chin that bore a day's stubble. The match died and was tossed aside. The man hooked his thumbs in his belt and sauntered down the line of servants, ignoring them.

He stopped in front of the duke, puffed on the cigar, and stared at the older man. Slowly, a pretense of a smile spread over his face. He removed the cigar from his mouth, shoved his hat back on his head, and spoke for the first time.

"Well, well, well. Evening, Daddy."

That accent, it was so strange—a hot, heavy drawl spiked with cool and nasty amusement. This man took his time with words, caressed them, savored them, and made his enemies wait in apprehension for him to complete them. The duke bristled, and his white hair almost stood out like a lion's mane as he gazed at his son.

"Jocelin, you forget yourself."

The cigar sailed to the ground and hissed as it hit the damp pavement. Liza longed to shrink back from the sudden viciousness that sprang from the viscount's eyes. The viscount smiled again and spoke softly, with relish and an evil amusement. The drawl vanished, to be supplanted by a clipped, aristocratic accent.

"I don't forget. I'll never forget. Forgetting is your vocation, one you've elevated to a sin, or you wouldn't bring my dear uncle where I could get my hands on him."

All gazes fastened on the man standing behind the duke. Though much younger than his brother, Yale Marshall had the same thick hair, black as his brother's had once been, only gray at the temples. Of high stature like his nephew, he reminded Liza of the illustrations of knights in *La Morte d'Arthur*, for he personified doomed beauty and chivalry. He had the same startling green eyes as his nephew, and he gazed at the viscount sadly as the younger man faced him.

Yale murmured to his brother, "I told you I shouldn't have come."

With knightly dignity he stepped aside, and the movement brought him nearer to his nephew. Jocelin's left hand touched the revolver on his hip as his uncle turned. The duke hissed his name, and the hand dropped loosely to his side. He lit another cigar.

At a glance from his face, the butler suddenly sprang into motion. He ran up the steps to open the door. The duke marched after him, leaving his son to follow, slowly, after taking a few leisurely puffs on his cigar.

"Ah, well," he murmured. "I can always kill him later."

SINS OF INNOCENCE
by
JEAN STONE

*They were four women with only one thing in common:
each gave up her baby to a stranger. They'd met in a
home for unwed mothers, where all they had to hold on
to was each other. Now, twenty-five years later, it's time
to go back and face the past. The date is set for a reunion
with the children they have never known. But who will
find the courage to attend?*

"I've decided to find my baby," Jess said.

Susan picked up a spoon and stirred in a hefty
teaspoon of sugar from the bowl. She didn't usually
take sugar, but she needed to keep her hands busy.
Besides, if she tried to drink from the mug now,
she'd probably drop it.

"What's that got to do with me?"

Jess took a sip, then quickly put down the mug.
It's probably still too hot, Susan thought. She probably burned the Estée Lauder right off her lips.

"I . . ." The woman stammered, not looking
Susan in the eye, "I was wondering if you've ever
had the same feelings."

The knot that had found its way into Susan's stomach increased in size.

"I have a son," Susan said.

Jess looked into her mug. "So do I. In fact, I have two sons and a daughter. And"—she picked up the mug to try again—"a husband."

Susan pushed back her hair. *My* baby, she thought. *David's baby.* She closed her eyes, trying to envision what he would look like today. He'd be a man. Older even than David had been when . . .

How could she tell Jess that 1968 had been the biggest regret of her life? How could she tell this woman she no longer knew that she felt the decisions she'd made then had led her in a direction that had no definition, no purpose? But years ago Susan had accepted one important thing: She couldn't go back.

"So why do you want to do this?"

Jess looked across the table at Susan. "Because it's time," she said.

Susan hesitated before asking the next question. "What do you want from me?"

Jess set down her mug and began twisting the ring again. "Haven't you ever wondered? About your baby?"

Only a million times. Only every night when I go to bed. Only every day as I've watched Mark grow and blossom. Only every time I see a boy who is the same age.

"What are you suggesting?"

"I'm planning a reunion. With our children. I've seen Miss Taylor, and she's agreed to help. She knows where they all are."

"*All* of them?"

"Yours. Mine. P.J.'s and Ginny's. I'm going to

contact everyone, even the kids. Whoever shows up, shows up. Whoever doesn't, doesn't. It's a chance we'll all be taking, but we'll be doing it together. *Together*. The way we got through it in the first place."

The words hit Susan like a rapid fire of a BB gun at a carnival. She stood and walked across the room. She straightened the stack of laundry. "I think you're out of your mind," she said.

And don't miss these heart-stopping
romances from Bantam Books,
on sale in March:

DARK PARADISE
by the nationally bestselling author
Tami Hoag
"Tami Hoag belongs at the top of
everyone's favorite author list"
—*Romantic Times*

WARRIOR BRIDE
by **Tamara Leigh**
" . . . a passionate love story that captures all
the splendor of the medieval era."
—nationally bestselling author
Teresa Medeiros

REBEL IN SILK
by **Sandra Chastain**
"Sandra Chastain's characters' steamy
relationships are the stuff dreams are
made of."
—*Romantic Times*

OFFICIAL RULES

To enter the sweepstakes below carefully follow all instructions found elsewhere in this offer.

The **Winners Classic** will award prizes with the following approximate maximum values: 1 Grand Prize: $26,500 (or $25,000 cash alternate); 1 First Prize: $3,000; 5 Second Prizes: $400 each; 35 Third Prizes: $100 each; 1,000 Fourth Prizes: $7.50 each. Total maximum retail value of Winners Classic Sweepstakes is $42,500. Some presentations of this sweepstakes may contain individual entry numbers corresponding to one or more of the aforementioned prize levels. To determine the Winners, individual entry numbers will first be compared with the winning numbers preselected by computer. For winning numbers not returned, prizes will be awarded in random drawings from among all eligible entries received. Prize choices may be offered at various levels. If a winner chooses an automobile prize, all license and registration fees, taxes, destination charges and, other expenses not offered herein are the responsibility of the winner. If a winner chooses a trip, travel must be complete within one year from the time the prize is awarded. Minors must be accompanied by an adult. Travel companion(s) must also sign release of liability. Trips are subject to space and departure availability. Certain black-out dates may apply.

The following applies to the sweepstakes named above:

No purchase necessary. You can also enter the sweepstakes by sending your name and address to: P.O. Box 508, Gibbstown, N.J. 08027. Mail each entry separately. Sweepstakes begins 6/1/93. Entries must be received by 12/30/94. Not responsible for lost, late, damaged, misdirected, illegible or postage due mail. Mechanically reproduced entries are not eligible. All entries become property of the sponsor and will not be returned.

Prize Selection/Validations: Selection of winners will be conducted no later than 5:00 PM on January 28, 1995, by an independent judging organization whose decisions are final. Random drawings will be held at 1211 Avenue of the Americas, New York, N.Y. 10036. Entrants need not be present to win. Odds of winning are determined by total number of entries received. Circulation of this sweepstakes is estimated not to exceed 200 million. All prizes are guaranteed to be awarded and delivered to winners. Winners will be notified by mail and may be required to complete an affidavit of eligibility and release of liability which must be returned within 14 days of date on notification or alternate winners will be selected in a random drawing. Any prize notification letter or any prize returned to a participating sponsor, Bantam Doubleday Dell Publishing Group, Inc., its participating divisions or subsidiaries, or the independent judging organization as undeliverable will be awarded to an alternate winner. Prizes are not transferable. No substitution for prizes except as offered or as may be necessary due to unavailability, in which case a prize of equal or greater value will be awarded. Prizes will be awarded approximately 90 days after the drawing. All taxes are the sole responsibility of the winners. Entry constitutes permission (except where prohibited by law) to use winners' names, hometowns, and likenesses for publicity purposes without further or other compensation. Prizes won by minors will be awarded in the name of parent or legal guardian.

Participation: Sweepstakes open to residents of the United States and Canada, except for the province of Quebec. Sweepstakes sponsored by Bantam Doubleday Dell Publishing Group, Inc., (BDD), 1540 Broadway, New York, NY 10036. Versions of this sweepstakes with different graphics and prize choices will be offered in conjunction with various solicitations or promotions by different subsidiaries and divisions of BDD. Where applicable, winners will have their choice of any prize offered at level won. Employees of BDD, its divisions, subsidiaries, advertising agencies, independent judging organization, and their immediate family members are not eligible.

Canadian residents, in order to win, must first correctly answer a time limited arithmetical skill testing question. Void in Puerto Rico, Quebec and wherever prohibited or restricted by law. Subject to all federal, state, local and provincial laws and regulations. For a list of major prize winners (available after 1/29/95): send a self-addressed, stamped envelope entirely separate from your entry to: Sweepstakes Winners, P.O. Box 517, Gibbstown, NJ 08027. Requests must be received by 12/30/94. DO NOT SEND ANY OTHER CORRESPONDENCE TO THIS P.O. BOX.